KT-404-299

Please return on or before the latest date above.
You can renew online at *www.kent.gov.uk/libs*
or by telephone 08458 247 200

CUSTOMER SERVICE EXCELLENCE **Libraries & Archives**

00884\DTP\RN\07.07   LIB 7

IN THE LINE
OF DUTY

IN THE LINE OF DUTY

BY

AMI WEAVER

Published in Great Britain 2013
by Mills & Boon, an imprint of Harlequin (UK) Limited.
Large Print edition 2014
Harlequin (UK) Limited, Eton House,
18-24 Paradise Road, Richmond, Surrey, TW9 1SR

© 2013 Ami Weaver

ISBN: 978 0 263 24012 2

Harlequin (UK) Limited's policy is to use papers that are natural, renewable and recyclable products and made from wood grown in sustainable forests. The logging and manufacturing processes conform to the legal environmental regulations of the country of origin.

Printed and bound in Great Britain
by CPI Antony Rowe, Chippenham, Wiltshire

For my wonderful editor, Carly Byrne.
Thank you, thank you, thank you,
for everything.

CHAPTER ONE

THE FIRST THING Matt Bowden had unpacked was the coffee machine, from the same box as his toothbrush, phone charger, a change of clothes and his dog's bowls. A guy had his priorities. And this morning, after he'd let Aldo, a German shepherd–God-only-knew-what mix, out in the backyard, he was glad he had planned ahead.

He inhaled deeply as he came back into the kitchen of the ranch house he'd rented and reached for a mug. Mmm. Coffee. He'd never thought he'd move back to his childhood city of Grand Rapids, Michigan. But when his former army buddy Brice and his wife, Marley, had called him with the offer of a partnership in an adventure tour company, and he'd just been discharged from the army, it seemed like a great fit. As a guy who loved very physical sports—kayaking, mountain biking, white-water rafting—it was perfect. So here he was. For now. He'd never been big on putting down roots, which was why army life suited him so well.

There wasn't much left for him here, and maybe that was a good thing. His mother had moved to Texas after Matt had joined up, straight out of high school, so with the exception of the very occasional wedding, he hadn't been back to Michigan in nearly twenty years.

He'd come back now because he owned part of a business. Matt shook his head. He'd never thought he'd end up here. He'd figured he had another ten years in the army in him, but after this brutal last tour in Kabul that plan had abruptly changed.

Barking caught Matt's attention as he poured his first cup of coffee. He frowned and set the mug on the counter. Odd. It sounded like his dog—except it was coming from the front of the house. Aldo was in the backyard. Matt wove his way through the unpacked boxes to the front door just in time to see his overfriendly dog leap at a red-haired woman across the street, planting his undoubtedly filthy paws on her chest.

With a curse, Matt wrenched open the door and raced outside in his socks. In March. Ignoring the cold and the slush, he ran down the driveway and across the street, yelling for Aldo. *Crazy mutt was nothing but trouble, and way too friendly.* Zeroing in on his dog, he didn't notice much about the woman, but he could almost feel the anger pouring off her. Not that he blamed her.

"Ma'am, I'm so sorry," he panted as he wrenched Aldo by the collar and got him to sit. "Somehow he got the back gate open. I must have not latched it properly." Matt lifted his gaze, then, to look at her. Past the muddy footprints on her shirt—over a nice pair of breasts, he couldn't help but notice; he was a guy, after all—to her face.

He stared at the red-haired woman in front of him. Her angry but beautiful features coalesced into a face he knew. Callie Marshall. *Wow.* His pulse gave a sharp kick and awareness stabbed him low in the gut.

And that was a completely inappropriate response to his childhood best friend's widow.

He recovered quickly. "Sorry, ma'am. Callie. He doesn't usually get away from me like that."

Aldo panted and sat on his foot, tongue lolling, eyes fixed on Callie.

She frowned at Matt and cocked her head. Her expression went from angry to puzzled to shocked, and she gave a little gasp as she stepped back. "Matt? Wait. You—I didn't know—you're the new neighbor?"

An unfamiliar awkwardness swamped him. "Yeah. I am. We are. I was planning on looking you up. How have you been?" The question seemed insufficient, given all she'd been through in the past year and half.

His friend's widow. God. Living across the street from him.

She gave him a tight smile. "I've been better. But thanks for asking." She brushed futilely at the mud on her shirt and his eyes zeroed right back in on her breasts.

Hell. He swallowed and forced his gaze away. "I'm sorry about your shirt. I'm not sure what came over Aldo. He's not usually so uncontrollable."

Her frown returned as her gaze shifted to Aldo. "I don't know if you know this, Matt, but I have two little kids. Lots of people around here do. We can't have an uncontrollable dog running around, knocking people down. It's not safe, for them or for your dog."

"I understand." He did. But did she really think he'd let his dog run around and hurt people? "He was excited. New neighborhood." To put it mildly; Aldo had come all the way from Afghanistan. And after the hell-and-back deployment they'd been through, Matt hadn't brought his buddy all the way here to have something happen to him.

She eyed Aldo. "I'm sure he was. But I've got to change now so I won't be late for work." She frowned as she looked at Matt's feet. "Seems like you might need some new socks."

He glanced down at his half-frozen feet. "Yeah. I was in a hurry. Again, I'm sorry, Callie."

"Just keep him under control. Nice to see you again, Matt." She turned and walked away, and he dragged his unrepentant pet back across the street and into the yard. While Matt wasn't sure if the dog had opened the gate or if it had come open on its own, he would replace the latch anyway. He shook the gate and noted how it wiggled. As soon as the hardware store opened, he'd pick something up. Callie was right. He couldn't have Aldo slipping out and jumping on people. Or getting hit by a car.

But Callie… He whistled and Aldo came loping back over, to follow him into the house. Matt had meant it when he'd said he planned on looking her up. Checking on her. He hadn't been able to be at the funeral. He'd been in the sandbox at the time. Jason's being gone still gave him a bad jolt whenever he thought of it, which was often.

But Matt hadn't planned on seeing her quite this soon. Or having her in his line of sight every day. She hadn't seemed any more thrilled to see him. Maybe the last thing she wanted was a reminder of her husband in *her* line of sight every day. If Matt had known she lived there, would he have rented a different house?

That didn't matter now.

He saw a dark blue minivan back out of the garage across the street. Aldo whined and shoved at Matt's hand with his nose. "What got into you? You should have left her alone, boy," he said as he rubbed Aldo's ears and watched her drive away. They'd done some training since he'd picked Aldo up from the rescue group that had gotten him home from Afghanistan, but the mutt had a long way to go. He tended to forget his manners—such as they were. But it'd been a long time since he'd jumped on someone like that. It was one of the first things Matt had worked on with him when they were still overseas.

As if they were on a loop, his thoughts returned to Callie. How was she doing? It was hard to tell from their unfortunate encounter, but from what he could see, the house was well cared for, so hopefully that meant she wasn't struggling. He'd thought of her occasionally over the past few months, and often of his old friend. He'd caught a glimpse of the kids yesterday morning when they'd been walked to a neighbor's. He'd thought nothing of it because he hadn't known whose kids they were.

Now he did, and things had shifted somehow.

* * *

Callie was still fuming when she left the house for the salon. It wasn't a Monday but it sure felt like one. The boys dragging their feet. The change of clothes when the bowl of cereal ended up in Liam's lap. The forgotten blankie—that was her fault, since in the cereal melee she'd forgotten to grab it from Liam's bed. Which was why she'd run back home to get it after taking the kids to Colleen's, only to have her shirt nearly ruined when she was jumped on by a huge dog with filthy paws.

Not to mention the shock of her life when Jason's old friend Matt Bowden had come racing out of the house across the street, yelling for the mutt. That had been what nearly knocked her over, not the dog. Which was apparently his.

She took a deep, shaky breath. Jason's friend. Matt was a link, however tenuous, to her husband. To her past. She wasn't quite sure how she felt about that. Oh, she ran into people all the time who'd known Jason, who'd been in her life before and after his death. But with one exception, none of them were people Jason had considered his best friend. Who'd known him his entire life.

Still. Callie hadn't really known Matt—he'd been sort of remote, but to be fair, they'd never really had a chance to get to know each other. She'd accepted him on faith, because he'd been Jason's friend. Since Matt had been in the military, it wasn't like there were backyard barbecues and time to get to know him. He'd been deployed when Jason, a firefighter, had died in the line of duty, and Matt hadn't been able to attend the funeral. He'd sent condolences, but that whole time was such a blur. Details kind of got lost in the haze of grief and disbelief that had shrouded everything for months.

She'd eventually emerged from that haze for the sake of her kids, but the shock of seeing Matt now threw her off balance. It would have been nice to be prepared, to know that he was moving in so close to her. But he'd seemed just as surprised to see her. To her knowledge, while he'd been in the States on leave, he hadn't been back to Grand Rapids at all. As far as not knowing who'd moved in, she and the kids had spent the weekend with Jason's parents, celebrating her father-in-law's birthday.

She had a little twinge of conscience. She'd been borderline rude to Matt. Yes, the dog had jumped on her. Yes, she was apparently having a bad day and it wasn't even nine in the morning yet. But that wasn't any reason to snap at him, when he'd been so clearly apologetic about the whole thing.

She pulled her van into her usual spot behind Time For You Salon and hurried in. Lori was behind the desk. "I'm sorry, Lori," she said, even though she'd called to let her know she was running behind.

"No problem," her friend and boss said. "You know that. What happened?"

Callie hung up her coat—somehow it had missed getting dirty—and filled her in on the morning. She downplayed Matt, but Lori must have picked up on some odd vibe.

"Hmm, a new neighbor. Single?"

Callie actually froze while reaching for a towel. She forced herself to move. "I have no idea, actually. He's an old friend of Jason's. I hadn't seen him for years, until today." That was the truth. Last she knew, Matt had been engaged. That had been several years ago, which most likely meant there was a wife by now. Matt had said "we" moved in. But Jason had never mentioned anything about a wedding. Callie would have thought he would have been in it, or at least sent a gift to the happy couple. Funny how she'd forgotten all about that until now.

"An old friend of Jason's. Well, well. We'll hope he's single," Lori said cheerfully, and Callie managed to recover enough to send her a mock glare. "Is he hot?"

Well, yeah, actually. She was astounded she'd actually noticed that, in all the commotion and her anger. But she easily recalled his broad shoulders, big hands, sweatpants stretched over muscular thighs, and ice-blue eyes. His eyes had always been striking. His hands on the dog had been firm but gentle. His brown hair was military short.

"I'll take that as a yes," Lori said, her voice smug, and Callie felt her face turn bright red. Damn her pale redhead's skin.

"I don't really know," she managed to reply. She'd gone for so long without really *seeing* another man that the whole idea of being attracted to one—a man who knew her husband, a man who wasn't her husband—caught her completely off guard and unsettled her. "The whole thing was kind of quick and I was really sort of focused on the dog and the mud."

"Understandable," Lori said. She sent Callie a sly look. "Maybe next time you see him you can check."

Callie laughed. "Or you can come over and check him out yourself."

Lori sent her an assessing look that made her uncomfortable. "Maybe I will."

The first of the day's clients came through the door then and Callie didn't get a chance to warn her friend off matchmaking. She'd decided it was better all around to raise her kids on her own, and besides, she didn't think she'd find anyone who could take Jason's place in her life. She couldn't imagine looking. It just seemed wrong. And if she ever was open to the possibility, it'd be with a guy who wasn't big on risk taking. She'd had enough of that for a lifetime. It for sure wouldn't be with a guy who'd been a friend of her husband's.

Who'd been a part of her wedding.

No, she wasn't taking any chances with her heart or her kids'.

Callie got through her day with no further mention of Matt, but he wasn't far from her thoughts. It made her irritable, but she tried to keep a lid on it. Her clients and now her kids didn't deserve to have her snappish. She pulled into her driveway and checked carefully for a big dog before she got out of the van. She'd been serious when she'd said she couldn't risk a badly behaved dog around her kids. He'd seemed friendly enough, just not well trained. Add it to the list of things she wasn't willing to chance.

Nothing jumped at her, so she hurried over to collect the boys from Colleen, her neighbor who ran an in-home day care.

"Hi, Callie," Colleen greeted her. "They're all ready for you. I noticed you met our new neighbor this morning."

"Ah. Yeah. Or his dog, rather," she said, plucking the kids' backpacks from their hooks.

Colleen made a little humming noise in her throat. "Mmm. If I wasn't married…"

Callie laughed. "But you are," she teased. She paused a second. "His name's Matt Bowden. He was a friend of Jason's."

The teasing look fell from Colleen's face. "Oh, Callie. I'm sorry."

She shook her head. "It's okay, really. I didn't know him that well. He's army. Or he was. I don't know if he's in anymore." She paused another second. Would he have moved into a house so far from an army base if he was still in? It didn't seem likely. "He and Jason were childhood friends." The words gave her a little pang. Did Jason's parents know he'd moved back? They hadn't said anything to her, and it seemed they'd have mentioned something about it. Since he and Jason had been such good friends.

"Are you going to be okay with that? With him?"

She gave Colleen a little smile. "I doubt I'll see him that much. But either way, it will be fine."

As long as he kept that dog of his under control. Otherwise, she had no intention of interacting with him beyond basic pleasantries and neighborliness. She could handle that. The kids didn't need to know him as their dad's friend.

Both boys burst into the foyer and greeted her with hugs, and the discussion of Matt was dropped.

In fact, she didn't think of him—much—during the predinner chaos at her own house. The promise of spring was in the air, enough so that she left the front door open, even though the glass was still up over the screen door. So when she looked out into the living room and saw her two little brown-haired boys clustered in front of the door, she frowned and went to see what they were looking at.

That dog was on the porch.

"Doggie!" Liam's squeal made her heart sink.

"Not our doggie," she said firmly, and looked past the dog to the house across the street. A light was on, and a car was in the driveway. The gate hung open. "Guys, give me some room. I'll take him back across the street."

"Can we come?" Eli asked eagerly, and Callie shook her head.

"But," she added at their crestfallen expressions, "you guys can stand on the porch. How's that?" That way they could see her and the dog, and she could keep an eye on them. Win-win. "Let me go first, so I can get hold of his collar." She didn't relish getting jumped on again, and she definitely wasn't willing to let the big mutt knock down one of her boys.

She edged out the door, speaking softly. "Hey buddy, stay right there." The dog perked right up, his tail wagging so hard his whole body shook. He made little whining noises in his throat and she held out a hand cautiously. He dropped to his belly and rolled right over. "No! I need you to get up. I need to take you home." She managed to get hold of his collar, and got him back on his feet. She gestured to the boys. "You can come out now," she said, and they did.

"Pat doggie?" Liam asked. His big blue eyes were fixed on the dog, and Eli was already edging closer.

"He's not very well trained," she began. But

then the dog sat on her foot, his eyes fixed on the kids, ears pricked. It'd probably be all right but… "He's not ours, guys, and I'm just going to take him home. Maybe another time."

"Where's he live?" Eli asked, and Callie pointed across the street.

"Just over there." *With your dad's friend*, she didn't add. Why was she so fixated on that fact?

She'd got the dog down the steps when Matt strode out onto the front porch of his house. "What the—Callie, I'm so sorry. Crazy mutt." He strode across the front lawn, shaking his head. "Aldo. How did you get out?"

The dog, Aldo, wagged his tail and barked.

"The gate's open," she said, and tried to withdraw her hand from the collar before the transfer. Touching Matt seemed almost dangerous. Still, his big hand brushed hers when he grasped the collar. The heat from that brief touch nearly had her stumbling back. She'd touched plenty of guys casually in the year and a half or so since her husband's death. A handshake, a haircut, an accidental bump in the grocery store. Never had she felt it like this.

She tucked her hand in her sweatshirt pocket, not wanting him to see her trembling fingers.

His chuckle was a low rumble and it reverberated…everywhere inside her. "So it is." He rubbed the top of the dog's head affectionately. Then he looked straight at Callie. Those ice-blue eyes seemed to pierce her soul. "I'm sorry, Callie. I'm not sure what the problem is here. But he likes you."

He almost sounded surprised. Callie stiffened. "Yeah, it's weird, isn't it? Hope you get that gate fixed. You don't want him to get hit by a car." She gave him a small smile and turned to go back home. Back where she'd be safe.

His hand on her arm stopped her.

"How old are they now?" The question was low, and his gaze was on Liam and Eli. In spite of herself, her heart gave a little tug. Of course, he'd see them as the kids of his childhood friend. It had to be hard on him—he hadn't been here for Jason's funeral, and for a while before that.

"Liam's three and Eli's five," she said. "And

I don't want them to decide to come over here. Have a good night."

She walked away and left Matt standing on the sidewalk, his misbehaving dog sitting on his foot.

CHAPTER TWO

MATT CLEARLY NEEDED a new solution. Aldo was determined not to be contained. The new latches on the gate weren't working. He'd gnawed his way through the kennel Matt had bought—basically chewed it to bits. And looked at Matt afterward as if to say *you should have known better*. No doubt the dog was right.

In the meantime, Matt took Aldo with him to work. Since he was more or less his own boss, it didn't matter. Letting Aldo bug Callie was wrong. Why the dog forgot all his manners—such as they were—and kept bothering her, he wasn't sure.

Seeing the boys last night had been a kick in the gut. They were so small, yet so big. He'd heard from Jason over the years he'd been gone, seen photos sent via email. *Too small*. Neither boy would remember his father that well. That made Matt's gut ache. He didn't remember his own father much, though his mother had tried to keep him alive for Matt. Unlike Jason, who'd died trying to save a friend and fellow firefighter in a fire, Matt's dad had not died a hero. He'd died a drunk.

How had he not known Callie lived across the street? Grand Rapids was a big city. He'd known Jason had moved house; they'd moved after Matt had deployed the last time. Needed more room with baby number two on the way. Since he and Jason had communicated through text messages and email, he probably hadn't asked for the address. It wasn't as if he'd sent Christmas cards from Afghanistan. Ironic that he'd been half a world away for so long, basically for his friend's entire marriage, and then ended up right across the street from his widow.

"So. Matt." Brice, his friend and partner, walked into Matt's cramped office after rapping his knuckles on the door frame. "What are you doing in here? I've been calling for you."

Matt thumped the chair legs down on the floor. Damn it. Considering the small size of the offices, he'd been thinking a little too hard about a certain pretty red-haired woman. That wasn't a good sign. He cleared his throat. "Sorry. Late night unpacking. What's up?"

His friend didn't push. In fact, they all kind of walked on eggshells around Matt since he'd been home from Afghanistan. He was fine; he had Aldo. The nightmares were few and far between. He didn't actually have PTSD—and he knew plenty of guys who did—but he did see the carnage of that last suicide bomber far too often when he closed his eyes. And he never talked about it. Period.

Brice held up a couple papers. "We've got a group that just signed up for a mountain biking trip. Four-day, U.P., Marquette. July. It's on your schedule. That going to be okay?"

Matt took the printout from Brice's hand, glad for the break from his useless thoughts. "More than. I love the Upper Peninsula. We're filling up nicely." This gave him no end of pride. They'd worked so hard to get Out There Adventures off the ground, running tours all over the Midwest, but especially in Michigan's Upper Peninsula, so it was a thrill to see more and more of the summer filling up. "If this keeps on, we may need to add another guide." They had five guides right now, including Matt, Brice and Brice's wife, Marley, but he could see them needing more. The whole thing was a bit of a risk—they went to the tour, rather than the tour coming to them—but so far it didn't seem to be deterring people from booking trips.

"Yeah." His friend stooped to rub Aldo's head. "Why is he here today?"

"Can't keep him in the backyard, and he's still not a fan of the kennel," Matt said, thinking of the destroyed kennel and the look on Callie's face when Aldo kept showing up. "He keeps bugging my neighbor. She's got little kids, and while I know he won't hurt them, she's understandably wary of him."

Aldo's tail thumped the floor and Brice laughed. "Animals are good at that—knowing who doesn't want them around—and homing in on that person."

"Yeah," he agreed. But Aldo's attachment to Callie was a little uncanny. The mutt went only to her house. Matt wasn't going to say that to Brice, however. "I'm going to look into heavy-duty latches for the gate. See if that helps. Something he can't head butt or paw at. That fenced-in backyard was the whole reason I rented the place to begin with. I don't want him to cause problems in the neighborhood or get hurt."

"Good luck with that. So this neighbor with the kids," Brice said a little too casually, as he sat on the corner of Matt's desk. "She single?"

He let out a bark of a laugh. "I don't have any idea." Because now that he thought about it, he didn't. And for some reason it bothered him. She wore wedding rings, but were those her rings from Jason, or someone new? As an old friend of Jason's, that didn't sit well with Matt, though of course she was entitled to move on with her life, and it was probably better if she did. Made no difference what he thought. But he wasn't going to admit to Brice he'd noticed the rings. He narrowed his eyes and pinned his married friend with a mock serious look. "Why? You looking? Marley know this?"

Brice shook his head. "Nope, I'm not interested. But you might be." He raised a brow.

Matt scrubbed a hand over his face. Damn ball lobbed right back in his court. "No. I'm not. Leave it alone, Bri. Please." Even if he was in the market for a relationship, it wouldn't be—couldn't be—Callie. His old friend's widow. It would be wrong. There was no way he was going to explain that to Brice.

His friend stood again, hands held up in front of him. "No harm done, my man. It was just a thought. You know, to bring you back to the world of the living."

"Of the happily married, you mean," Matt said, but there was no heat in his tone. He didn't begrudge his friend his happy marriage, or his wanting Matt to have the same. He envied him a little, especially because he knew if he'd married his ex-fiancée their marriage would never have gone the way Brice's had. That had been a mistake from start to finish, and had only underscored what Matt had already known—he was better off alone. Her accusations that he was commitment-shy, even after she had received the engagement ring, hadn't been too far off the mark. He was smart enough to know his limits.

Brice smiled lazily. "Yep. And all the perks that go along with it."

Matt shook his head and Brice left the room, his comically evil laugh floating behind him. Instead of dwelling on what he'd meant—something Matt had been without for too long now—he opened up the equipment spreadsheet and focused on work, not his sadly lacking love life.

Callie pulled the chicken breasts she'd been thawing all day out of the fridge just as Eli burst into the kitchen.

"Mom, can me and Liam play with Legos?"

She gave him a quick smile. "Sure. But use the big ones only, not the little ones, please." Liam was pretty good about not putting things in his mouth anymore, but she wasn't taking any chances. He was only three, after all.

"Okay!" Eli called as he dashed back into the living room. "We can," she heard him say, and she couldn't help but smile. She pulled a knife from the butcher block holder and started slicing.

Matt flashed into her head and she put the knife down. She didn't want to accidentally cut her finger off if she wasn't concentrating fully on what she was doing. She wasn't sure what to make of this weirdness. It wasn't just that he was Jason's friend—it was these strange feelings he aroused inside her. Maybe it was a signal she was finally moving into another stage of grief? Not really moving on, because she wasn't sure she'd ever be completely ready to move on, but acknowledging she was a woman with needs and feelings?

Well, except she didn't want to have needs and feelings. They complicated everything, and she was looking to keep her focus on her kids only. Getting distracted by a guy wasn't going to allow her to do that.

Would Jason want you to be both parents to the boys? She inhaled sharply at the little voice, then picked up the knife and resumed slicing chicken. She didn't know what he'd want, but if she were honest with herself, she knew he wouldn't want her to wallow forever in grief.

A crash sounded from the living room as blocks hit the ground, closely followed by loud little-boy laughter. It made her smile. No, she wasn't wrong to keep her focus on her boys. Not at all. They wouldn't be small forever and she was right to keep them at the center of her world.

Her phone rang. A quick glance at the display revealed it to be her mother. Jean lived in Florida, but she checked in with her often. Callie washed her hands quickly and grabbed the phone.

"Hi, Mom," she said, tucking the phone under her ear and reaching for a skillet. "How is warm, sunny Florida?"

Her mother's laugh rolled over the connection. "Neither warm nor sunny at the moment, but no doubt still nicer than Michigan in March."

Callie flicked her gaze out the kitchen window, over the melting snow, the patchy brown grass that would soon be mud, and the bare branches. While she'd never regretted moving to Michigan with Jason, some days she missed her native Florida. "You'd be right."

They chatted for a minute, then Callie said, "I've got to get something going on the stove. I'm going to give you to Eli and Liam."

It took only a moment to set them up on speaker,

and she returned to the kitchen to get the chicken going. When she went back out to the living room, she heard them all laughing, and wished her mom could be closer. She had, in fact, urged Callie to move back home. But somehow the idea of leaving behind this place where she'd made a life with Jason—even to return to her child-hood home—was too much. They'd come here because he'd always wanted to be a firefighter in Grand Rapids, like his dad before him. She'd been happy to accommodate his dream. Now he was gone, but she and her sons were firmly set-tled in. She didn't want to uproot them now.

"Okay, guys, it's my turn. Say bye to Grandma."

They did with a loud chorus, and Callie picked the phone up. "What did they talk about? Legos?"

"Mmm, somewhat. But mostly about a dog. And a guy."

"Matt?" Callie's mind went completely blank. And when it clicked back in, she realized she'd made a crucial mistake. But still—the boys had noticed Matt? Why? They hadn't even talked to him. Her mom, of course, pounced on her slip.

"They didn't tell me his name. Who is he, Callie? Are you dating someone?" There was no censure in her mother's voice, only a gentle curiosity. Horror rushed through Callie, followed by a sort of emptiness.

"No. No, of course not, Mom. Why would I do that?" She tried to keep her tone light, keep this conversation from going any further.

Jean's sigh carried over the connection. "Why wouldn't you? It's not a bad thing, Callie. You're young. Gorgeous. There's no reason you can't love again."

Callie let out a little laugh, but it sounded forced. "Of course there is. I loved my husband, Mom. I'd never—I'd just never." Especially with a man who'd been his friend.

"Well, no, of course you wouldn't if he were alive, honey," Jean said. "But you don't have to be alone now he's gone. He would never want you to be alone. If he'd been able to make sure you were taken care of, he would have."

A powerful sorrow pressed on Callie's chest. "I can take care of us."

"Of course you can. And you do. You do a wonderful job of it. But who takes care of you, Callie? And don't say you do," she added. "I'm not talking physical care of yourself and you know it. I'm talking emotional. A partner to share the day to day with. You don't have to be alone. I haven't wanted to say anything, but since this is the first time the boys have mentioned anyone outside of your little circle, I thought I'd ask."

Callie stabbed at the chicken with the spatula, barely able to see the skillet through her tears. "I'm fine, Mom," she said, even though the thickness of her voice with the tears belied her words. She swallowed hard. "I take care of myself just fine. And Matt is our new neighbor. He's got a dog that keeps escaping." She didn't mention the dog kept coming to her house. Or that Matt was—well, Matt.

"Is he young? Available?"

Now Callie had to laugh at the hope in her mother's voice. "I don't know how old he is, Mom. Older than me, I'd guess, but not by much. And I'm not interested enough to know if he's available. He's not interested in me. At all." Was that too much protesting? Goodness. She shook her head. Good thing her mother couldn't see her.

Jean made a little noise. "Too bad. Just don't close yourself off from possibilities. Promise me, Callie. Maybe it's not this man, but if one comes along, don't hide from it."

"I've got the boys to think about," she pointed out, slightly peeved that her mother didn't focus on that. "I'm not going to risk upending their lives for—for a chance, Mom. For something that probably won't even work out. That's selfish and not fair to them. They've lost so much already."

"I know, honey." Her mother's voice was gentle. "You're nothing if not responsible. But don't you think it'd be good for them to see you happy?"

Callie took a sharp breath. Her mother's words hit her hard. "I'm happy. As happy as I can be, considering."

"Well, right. But like I said, they deserve to see you taken care of. They are going to want to take that on themselves in a few years. Do you want them to feel responsible for you, too? Shouldn't they know it's okay to be happy, too? It's not like you'd cut Jason out of the picture. He'll always be their father. Always. You being happy with another man doesn't take that from them, or take away anything from Jason's memory."

Those words struck deep. Callie sighed. While part of her knew her mother was right, part of her resisted it so hard because it was a step into the unknown. And it seemed silly as an adult to be afraid of the unknown. But she controlled what she could, and right now she kept everything as safe as she could for her little family. With as little risk to them as possible. Bringing in someone new—even Matt— ran the risk of upending everything and leaving them swinging in the breeze again if he should decide to leave. She'd been through the soul-sucking pain of loss already. She wasn't risking going back to that.

"I appreciate your concern," she said carefully. "But I think I've got everything under control. I can't make any promises about possibilities, Mom, but I will try. I think that's all I can do right now."

There was the slightest of pauses. "Then that's all I can ask for. I love you, honey. I just want what's best for you."

"I love you, too," Callie said. "And I know you

do." She hoped her mother wouldn't push this, wouldn't keep at her to pursue something she wasn't in any way ready for. Wasn't sure she'd ever be ready for.

"I'll let it go," Jean said, in a voice that made it clear she didn't want to, and Callie had to smile. "But I'm still hopeful, honey."

"You can be," Callie said, because it would make her mom feel better.

They said their goodbyes and hung up. Callie put the phone on the counter and sighed. She couldn't very well tell the boys not to talk about Matt. They'd noticed him right away and they didn't usually pick up on strangers like that. It unnerved her, especially given her own unwelcome attraction to him. It was like something in all of them recognized him in a way, on a level she didn't want to examine too closely.

Or it could just be as simple as the man had a dog and her boys wanted one, too.

She laughed at herself as she pulled the chicken off the stove. She'd go with the latter, since they were little boys, and the possibility of anything else was far too uncomfortable.

* * *

More snow.

Callie stared out the kitchen window the next morning at the white stuff blanketing the driveway. A good six inches rested on the railing of the porch. Snow in March wasn't unheard of, but the weatherman hadn't said there'd be measurable snow. And this was the thick, heavy stuff, not the light and fluffy lake effect they often got. She did quick calculations in her head. It'd take her a good twenty minutes to shovel the driveway. Another ten or so to do the sidewalk. And she had to be ready to leave in forty.

Standing there wishing it'd just go away wasn't helping.

With a sigh, she threw on her winter gear and trudged outside. The snow was pretty, a temporary cover on the dingy snow piles and the patchy brown grass, but that wasn't going to last long. Already it was melting, dripping from the eaves of her house. Grabbing her shovel—darn it, she'd really hoped she was done with the thing for this year—she got ready to get to work, then heard the whine of a snowblower across the street.

A quick peek revealed Matt out clearing his driveway. Callie allowed herself a moment of pure, unadulterated snowblower envy. Jason had always enjoyed the physical act of shoveling. Something that Callie had never understood, but she hadn't argued, since he got it done. Now he was gone and the task fell to her.

She heaved a shovelful of the heavy stuff to the side of the driveway. Maybe she should go find one on sale for the end of the season. Jason would shake his head at her and give her that full-on grin. *Why are you doing this, Cal?* Some days the memories hurt. Others, they were bittersweet. Today, she smiled a little at his voice in her head.

Callie dumped another shovel load and looked up. The sound of the machine was getting closer. Matt was coming across the street—which wouldn't get plowed for hours, if ever—toward her house. She leaned on her shovel and couldn't help but notice how gorgeous he was in well-fitting jeans, a navy down vest over a gray sweatshirt, and a colorful knit hat. Guilt hit her at once—though it wasn't his fault, darn it—and she frowned when he stopped in front of her. "Can I help you?"

"That's what I was going to ask *you*. Can I help you with this?" He gestured at the driveway with one gloved hand. "It won't take long."

Callie accidentally caught his ice-blue gaze and her breath snagged. Heat rose in her face. She looked away and cleared her throat. "I've got it. Thanks, though."

Right then the front door burst open. "Mom! I dropped the milk on the floor!" Eli's voice was half-hysterical. Callie squeezed her eyes shut.

"Hang on," she called back. "I'll be right there." She gave Matt a weak smile. "Kids."

"Callie. Let me do this for you while you tackle the milk." There was a quiet humor in his voice and part of her wanted to respond to it. She bit her lip, then nodded. There was no rational reason to turn him down. *You make my insides do funny things* didn't count as an excuse.

"Okay. That'd be great. Thank you." Despite her best intentions, the words came out sounding stiff.

He didn't seem to notice. "No problem." He

turned back to the snowblower and Callie hurried as best she could though the snow to the garage. She'd been thrown off kilter wasn't fully sure why Matt made her feel this way. She'd seen plenty of attractive men since Jason died. Many of them had known her husband. None of them—not a single one—had registered with her until Matt. It worried and annoyed her.

"Eli," she said when she entered the kitchen, shedding her gloves and coat, and noting the large puddle on the floor. "What happened in here?"

He looked up at her out of her husband's eyes. Blue, as well, but more of a denim rather than the startling crystal-blue of Matt's. "It kinda fell."

"I see that." It had been a nearly full gallon. Usually she poured some into a smaller container to make it easier for Eli to use, but she'd forgotten about that in her hurry to shovel the driveway. "If your socks are wet, go ahead and change them while I clean this up. Is Liam up yet?"

"I don't know. Liiiam," he yelled as he ran out of the kitchen, and Callie laughed in spite of herself. If Liam hadn't been awake before, he would be now.

She cleaned up the milk and threw the sopping towels into the washer in the basement. When she came back up, she looked out and realized Matt had finished not only the driveway but the sidewalk, as well. Now she owed him thanks, which meant she'd have to talk to him and risk that little frisson of—something. That little something that reminded her, just barely, that she wasn't just a mom and a young widow—she was a woman.

CHAPTER THREE

ALDO HADN'T BEEN thrilled with the snow. He'd been what Matt would normally consider a big baby, and getting him to do his business had been a bit of an ordeal. But he didn't blame the poor guy. Clearly, Aldo hadn't forgotten his last winter in Afghanistan, which he'd spent half-starved, with frostbitten ears and shredded paws. So Matt had shoveled a path to the spot his furry friend preferred, and waited while the dog had done his business. Quickly.

On the other hand, there was no way the mutt would make a break for Callie's in the snow.

Callie. She hadn't been too happy to have him clear her driveway. Was it him, or help in general she wasn't keen on? Hard to know. But the question bugged him all day, in the back of his mind. He got held up and didn't leave until late—Brice had a wife to get home to, and Matt, well, didn't—so he really didn't mind. He drove home through the wet streets and pulled into his driveway.

When he got out, he looked back and saw Callie coming down the porch steps. This gave him an unwelcome little jolt. He shut the truck door to keep Aldo inside for a minute, then walked to the end of his driveway and waited, unable to keep his eyes off her. Her curls were up in a clip; in the pale glow of the streetlight he could see it was slightly lopsided, as if she'd thrown it up quickly. She was wearing yoga pants, big fluffy boots and a worn, oversize sweatshirt.

She was sexy as hell.

Trying to bring his thoughts back around to more mundane matters, he asked, "You okay?"

She crossed her arms tightly under her breasts. The defensive posture made him wonder if it was the cold or his presence that made her uncomfortable. Possibly both. "I just wanted to say thank you for your help this morning. But normally I can handle it."

"Of course you can," he said, and wondered

why she felt the need to warn him off. Why it mattered so much to her.

She nodded and her gaze caught his, then slid away. Just like earlier. Why was it so hard for her to make eye contact with him? Was he that scary? Or was it his past with Jason that bothered her?

"Some days are a little crazy," she said, with an awkward little laugh.

"I bet," he said, thinking of his own childhood without a father. His mother had done her best, but it hadn't been easy raising two boisterous boys, though they'd both turned out okay in the end.

"Okay. I just wanted you to know." She started backing up and Matt automatically took a step back, as well, to give her space. He was fairly sure this was the first time he'd had a woman run away from him. It was a bit of a blow to the ego, but hey, he was a big boy. He'd get over it. He watched as she turned and hurried back to her house. Her long sweatshirt fell to her thighs. It was too bad it covered the rear view. Shame burned through him. What kind of guy checked out his buddy's widow's backside? God. He turned around and walked back to the car to let Aldo out. The dog whined and tugged the leash in the direction of Callie's house.

"Sorry, boy," Matt murmured. "She's off-limits."

Callie shut the door behind her and leaned on it, trying to calm her leaping pulse. That had been a mistake. For one thing, it looked as if she'd been waiting for him, which, okay, maybe she had, but not in the way he might think. And the worst part was she really did find him seriously attractive.

She covered her face with her hands. All she had to do was ignore it. Ignore him. Ignore the links he represented to her husband. Denial, denial, denial. It would go away. It wasn't that hard. This morning she'd been stressed. Right now she was tired. She could rationalize until she was purple, but the fact remained that every time she was near Matt her nerves did this bizarre little dance. It scared the heck out of her.

She hadn't even touched him. What would happen then?

She pushed herself off the door and made

her way to her bedroom, turning off lights as she went. Nights weren't her favorite. Eli had frequent nightmares related to losing his dad, though it had been a while since the last one. She knocked lightly on the wooden door frame as she entered her room. Hopefully, that streak would continue. Sometimes she simply couldn't sleep. Part of her was always waiting for another middle-of-the-night phone call. Plus, with the kids needing her, there was no way to take any kind of sleep medicine, though she did have a prescription for one she'd never filled.

Her bed was so big. Lonely.

She pulled Jason's old sweatshirt over her head and dropped it on the chair in the corner before crawling into bed and pulling the covers up to her chin. She was *supposed* to be lonely. She'd come to accept the feeling as a friend, in a way. It was familiar now. A reminder of what she'd lost. She missed Jason. She'd miss him every day for the rest of her life. But the kids kept her busy and were such a blessing. She was making a new life. One that included only them, not an outsider who, as she'd told her mother, might leave them shattered if he chose to walk away.

Callie was done taking risks. Not with her kids, not with her life and not with her heart. She couldn't take any more loss. She'd give up whatever she had to in order to keep them all safe.

That meant keeping her distance from Matt, because as long as he made her feel like this, he was most definitely not safe.

Unfortunately for her decision to stay away, Matt pulled into his driveway the next evening as she was walking back with the kids from Colleen's. Both boys immediately went bug-eyed.

"Maybe we can see the dog, Mom," Eli said excitedly, and slid a look at Liam. *Uh-oh.* Had they been conspiring over a way to meet Aldo? She wouldn't put it past them. They were pretty determined when they were in accord.

So she made a noncommittal noise. "Come on, guys, let's get inside," she urged, but they were still both staring when Matt got out of his truck. So was she, but for a completely different reason. Watching him unfold his long frame made her pulse flutter. Goodness. She swallowed. "Boys," she said in her best warning tone, then wondered who the warning was really for—her or them?

"We wanna see the dog," Eli said, and Liam nodded firmly.

Matt sent a grin in their direction from across the street before Callie could say anything. "Hey, guys," he called as he started toward them. "You want to pet Aldo? If it's okay with your mom," he added, with a look at Callie.

She stepped up quickly and spoke over their chorused "yes!"

"You just got home. I'm sure you have other things to do."

"It's no problem," he said, crossing the street, Aldo at his side. Matt's eyes held hers, and Callie couldn't suppress a little shiver.

The boys spun to her and tugged on her coat. "Please, Mom?" Eli begged, his eyes big.

Everything in her screamed to say no. But that had nothing to do with a dog or the kids. It wasn't fair to punish the boys because she had issues with the dog's handsome owner. She relented reluctantly. "Okay. But only for a minute."

Matt shot her a slightly lopsided grin. *That wasn't so hard, was it?* it seemed to say.

You have no idea, she wanted to answer. The whole idea of being around him threw her off balance. And she definitely could not allow her kids to develop a relationship with him. That would be dangerous. He'd move on and the boys would be hurt, and she wasn't putting them through that again.

And she was way ahead of herself. All they were doing was petting a man's dog.

Matt and Aldo came up on the sidewalk. The snow was melting, but she noticed the dog took care not to step in the spots where it remained.

"Eli and Liam, this is Mr. Bowden." She laid a hand on each boy's head as she said their names. She did not say Matt had known their dad. No sense in muddying the waters. Aldo leaned forward on his leash, tail wagging hard.

"Nice to meet you, Eli and Liam," Matt said, as he shook each boy's hand. "But please call me Matt. This is Aldo. He's very friendly. He'd love to have you pet him."

Both boys, eyes huge, reached out and touched

Aldo's dark coat. "Hi, doggie," Liam said softly, and Callie's heart squeezed. She'd never hear the end of this from them.

"He's so soft," Eli said wonderingly. Matt crouched down and slid an arm around Aldo's neck, and the dog sat down, tail still going. Matt was on the boys' level now.

"He is," he agreed. "And he's got a very special story. Want to hear it?"

Both boys nodded, and something kept Callie quiet.

"Aldo came from all the way across the world. We found him last year when I was in Afghanistan. Our army unit sort of adopted him." Matt glanced up at Callie, then touched one of Aldo's ears. "He was in very bad shape and needed some serious help. We found him on the streets."

Callie could see, now, the damage on the dog's ears, and she reached out and rubbed his head, as her boys were doing. A rescue dog, for sure, but not like she'd expected.

"We worked hard to save him and get him healthy again. When I got out of the army, I worked with a rescue group to bring him home with me. He's been here just a few months. And he's not a fan of the snow, but he loves kids. I couldn't—I couldn't leave him there." While his tone was light, Callie saw the emotion in his expression.

"He's okay now?" Eli asked, his eyes big.

"Yep. Just fine," Matt assured him, and her heart flipped a little. The man had moved heaven and earth to bring this dog home. Callie ran her hand over Aldo's head. A man who'd spend that kind of money and time to save a dog half a world away—no, not just a dog, but his friend—was a good man.

"So his training's been a little spotty, but we're working on it," Matt said as he stood up. His words were directed at Callie now. "I know he keeps bugging you, and I'm not sure why."

Now, after a glimpse of what he'd been through, she felt bad for getting angry with Aldo. "He must know my kids want a dog. Animals are good like that," she suggested with a slight smile. "How long did it take to get him here?"

Matt shoved his hands in his pockets. "Four months. A lot of people did a lot of work to bring him home, and other dogs like him. Cats, too. They're still doing it, but funds are an issue. It's a miserable, miserable thing, to be an animal on the streets there."

She didn't doubt it. "You saved him."

"You can't save everyone," he said quietly. She reached out on impulse, and laid her hand on his arm, wishing she could erase the haunted look from his eyes, wondering what he'd seen. He didn't look at her, but he did touch her hand with his free one. She snatched hers back and tucked it in her pocket. Time to change the subject and break the sense of intimacy.

She cleared her throat. "He's great with kids. Whoa, Liam, we can't sit on the dog, honey. Pats only."

Matt slid her a sideways glance. "You said they want a dog?"

Callie sighed. "Yes. Of course they do." Didn't all little boys?

"Not happening?"

She shook her head. "We're gone all day. That's a long time for an animal to be alone. I'd hate to kennel him or her, and I'd be responsible for walking, feeding, cleaning up. The boys are not big enough to do that themselves yet, and I have enough chores to see to as it is. So, no dog for us."

"Makes sense." Matt didn't press or make her feel judged for turning down her kids' fondest wish. "I had a dog when I was a little older than Eli. Jason always wanted one. He bugged his parents relentlessly."

The casual mention of her husband had her gaze shooting to his. Matt was watching her closely, clearly aware he'd crossed an invisible line she'd drawn. *No mention of my husband.* She swallowed.

"I know. His parents told me."

Matt took a step closer and inclined his head so he couldn't be heard over the boys' giggling. The closeness raised goose bumps on her arms that had nothing to do with the March chill. "I'm not sure what I'm supposed to say—or not say—about Jason. He was my best friend growing up. I have stories about him that your boys might like to hear. But I don't want to overstep any boundaries. It's totally up to you."

Callie looked down at the sidewalk. He had a

point. Letting him in meant he'd be in her life, her kids' lives, with all the associated risks. She wasn't sure how she felt about that. Still, was it fair to use her mixed feelings to prevent them from learning more about their dad?

Of course not.

Knowing what she did now—that he'd moved heaven and earth to save a dog—she realized she viewed Matt in a slightly different light. She'd been trying to keep him at arm's length. Looking for a reason to do it, to hold him away, to try to keep these jumbled, unwelcome feelings at bay. The story about Aldo had taken a chunk out of her resolve.

It didn't mean she had to do anything about these weird feelings. They'd probably go away on their own, anyway.

So she'd let him spend limited time with her boys. It would be good for all of them.

"Can you—can you come over for dinner? Tomorrow?" The words fell out in a rush, before she lost her nerve. "It's not a date. Just to spend a little time with the kids. It won't be fancy. I'll make mac and cheese. From scratch. Or I can do something else." Realizing she was babbling, she fell silent, and wished the earth would swallow her up. Why had she blurted out that it wasn't a date? Of course it wasn't.

He held her gaze. "I like mac and cheese. And I accept your kind invitation."

"Okay." She nodded. Why on earth had she said the *d* word? "We eat early—what time do you get home?"

"I can be home by five-thirty," he said.

"So, say, by six? That's as late as I can hold the boys off," she said.

"That's fine."

She looked at Aldo, who was happily lapping up the love from her boys. "He can come, too. If he's well behaved."

Matt flashed her that grin she was starting to dread, because it made parts of her weak that had no business being weak. "He is."

"Okay, then. All right, guys, time to go home and get a snack."

"Miss Colleen gave us one before we left, and you say we can only have one snack before dinner," Eli pointed out, and Callie ground her teeth together. Every single other day, they wanted a snack every five minutes. Today, when she was willing to use it as a bribe, they failed her.

Matt shot her a look of amusement. "Your mom's saying it's time to go," he said smoothly, and she sighed. Apparently she was transparent, as well. "And I've got to get Aldo home, too."

"Can we take him for a walk sometime?" Eli asked hopefully.

Callie frowned at him. "Eli! Where are your manners?"

He frowned back at her, then brightened. "Please?"

Matt started to cough, which Callie guessed was an attempt to hide a laugh. Her own lips twitched in spite of herself. "While that's better, I meant that we don't just invite ourselves along. And it's time to go home. We haven't even made it into the house yet and we've been gone all day." To Matt she said, "Thanks for bringing Aldo over. They clearly enjoyed it."

He sent her a slow smile, as if he knew she was running away. "I don't mind." He gave Aldo a tug on the leash and the dog stood up reluctantly. "See you tomorrow."

"Yeah, see you," she muttered as he walked away. She did not watch him go. Instead, she herded her boys up the sidewalk and into their own house. The usual winter chaos of shedding coats and boots and backpacks, and hanging everything up where it should go, made her feel as if she had four kids instead of two.

But it wasn't enough to distract her from the fact she'd invited Matt to dinner.

"I want a dog like Aldo," Eli said wistfully the next morning, and Callie sighed. This was the hundredth time since last night she'd heard them mention a dog.

"I know, sweetie. But we can't take care of one right now. Did you brush your teeth?" When he nodded too swiftly, because she knew him so well, she pressed, "With toothpaste?"

He shot her a look that said *busted* and headed back to the bathroom. Callie couldn't help but grin. He was a sneaky one, her Eli. She had to be very specific when it came to things he didn't particularly enjoy. According to her mother-in-law, Jason had been the same way as a child.

Callie helped Liam get dressed and took him in to brush his teeth, as well. "Doggie?" he asked hopefully, and she tapped him under the chin, looking into his big brown eyes.

"Not right now." To redirect him, and try to avoid a meltdown, she asked, "Is Mr. P in your backpack?"

He trotted off in search of the stuffed penguin. Callie shut her eyes for just a moment and leaned on the vanity. She was going to have to do something to shut down this dog thing. It was so hard to say no to them, but as she'd told Matt, they were gone almost all day. That wasn't good for a dog. They could probably manage a cat, but even that she felt guilty about. And none of it was easy to explain to little kids.

Everything gathered, she herded the boys out the door and over to Colleen's. Callie left them with hugs and kisses, and headed to work.

There had been a time when she and Jason had discussed opening her own salon. After the kids were a little bigger, they'd agreed. Well, they were bigger, and she still hadn't taken the strides to pursue the dream. Wasn't sure if she wanted to anymore. Wasn't sure why she wouldn't want to.

Lori knew it had been in her future plans, but didn't press her in any way. She'd never discouraged her dream, but had stated she'd hate to lose Callie as an employee. And it was comfortable, working at the Time For You Salon. The routine, the clients she loved, Lori as her friend and boss. None of it involved any real risk to herself, that could end up with her and her boys on the street if she failed. There was no Jason with a financial safety net to fall back on if it didn't work out.

So she'd filed the dream away.

And tried to ignore the little twinge of regret.

"She said it wasn't a date? Interesting," Marley commented, and exchanged a glance with Brice.

Matt looked up at his friend's wife—and fellow guide—sharply. "Why do you say that?"

"Because if she has to frame it as a non-date, she was thinking of it as a date." When he blinked at her, Marley leaned over and smacked his arm lightly. "Matt. Follow along. She's making her boundaries clear. She's doing that because either she's getting vibes from you or she's trying to convince herself it's what she wants."

He tipped his chair back. "I've never gotten any vibes from her." Not true. She'd been giving off stay-back vibes from day one. She'd all but busted out a cross and garlic. But that was a blow to the ego he didn't need to share.

Marley raised a brow. "Then you're giving them off."

Matt shook his head. "I don't think so, Marley. I knew her husband. We were neighbors, best friends when we were kids. I was in their wedding, for God's sake. So no. There are no vibes." How stupid was he to bring it up to Marley? When she'd invited him to dinner with her and Brice, he should have said no and left it at that, instead of saying he was going to Callie's.

Marley looked at him for a long moment, then shook her head. "She feels threatened by something or she wouldn't lay it out straight like that. And no wonder. All that history with her husband. Is she going to…" She paused.

"Is she going to what?"

"Confuse you with him?"

Matt's gut clenched. "I don't think so. Jason and I, we were nothing alike."

The phone rang and Marley got up to answer it. "Just be careful."

Her words rang in his head after she left. Was Callie feeling threatened by something? What it could be, he didn't know. The only real contact they'd had centered around Aldo, and a couple brief and awkwardly polite conversations. Nothing truly personal. Sure, he found her appealing and was definitely attracted to her, but he wasn't going to let on or act on it. She was as off-limits as a woman could get. And he wasn't interested in getting involved with her, anyway.

Was he?

CHAPTER FOUR

CALLIE STARED AT the mess in the living room the next evening. It sure hadn't taken long for Eli and Liam to make it appear as though a tornado had slammed through their toys. It didn't matter, it didn't matter, she chanted in her head. This was just a friendly dinner. Still. She couldn't help herself. "Boys, can you please put the Legos back in the boxes? We don't want Mr. Bowden to step on them." Or the dog to eat them, for that matter. She'd let them leave the plastic containers in the living room. To have it too clean was to risk having him think she'd gone to a lot of trouble for him and *it was just a friendly dinner.*

Clearly, she had some issues.

The clatter of the plastic blocks hitting the boxes followed her into the kitchen. She'd made mac and cheese as promised. From scratch, using her mother's recipe. It was a dish the kids loved, and it smelled divine. She had the fixings for a salad, as well. The whole meal was pretty easy, which was good, because she kept getting distracted by the thought of Matt in her house, sitting at her table.

Deep breath.

The timer went off, five minutes before he was due to arrive. She pulled the steaming dish out of the oven and placed it carefully on the stove top.

"Is it ready, Mama? We're hungry," Eli said, standing a safe distance from the oven.

"Almost," she said with a smile. "Why don't you guys wash up and then he should be here. We'll eat right after that."

"All right!" Eli shouted as he turned and headed back to Liam. Callie's smile slipped. Was she doing the right thing, bringing this man into her children's lives? What if they got attached, something happened and he had to leave? She had no reason to think he was staying. Hadn't Jason said the army suited Matt because he didn't like being tied down?

"Just a friendly dinner," she mumbled to herself, and her pulse jumped when the doorbell rang. She laid a hand on her belly and took a deep breath to settle her nerves as she walked to the door. She pulled it open and flat-out forgot to breathe. He wore jeans and a plaid oxford shirt, and smelled so good she thought she'd tip forward right into him. Aldo stood next to him, tail wagging like crazy. He had a spiffy blue bandanna tied around his neck.

"Hi," she said, and sounded only a little breathy.

"Hi." His voice was amused, and she snapped out of her idiocy and stepped back as the boys came running into the room. He held a bakery box. "Cookies from The Sweet Stop. I figured that was better than wine, what with the kids and all. That okay?"

She accepted the box and shut the door behind him. A glass of wine might very well have taken the edge off this evening. But she was truly touched by his thoughtfulness. "Perfect. The kids'll love them. Thank you."

The boys came closer. Eli zeroed in on the bakery box. "Oh, look, Liam! Cookies!" Identical pleading gazes swung from the box to her face. "Can we have one?"

"Not until after dinner," she told them, and nodded to Matt. "You can put your coat on the back of the chair there. Aldo is welcome to hang out here."

"Can we pet him?" Eli asked, and Matt nodded, unsnapping the leash.

"Sure." He grinned as both boys practically fell on the dog.

"Good thing I had them wash up for dinner," Callie said with a rueful little laugh as she started for the kitchen.

"Oh." Matt stopped, looked back, chagrin clear on his face. "Sorry. I didn't think about that."

Of course he hadn't; he wasn't a parent. "It's fine. Sit down, guys," she called over her shoulder. "You can pet him after we eat." To Matt she added, "You can have a seat."

But he followed her into the kitchen. "I can't let you serve me," he said, when she turned to protest. He stood so close, all she could smell was his scent. His words were teasing, but his eyes were—well, not so much. There was a heat in them she wasn't ready for. She swallowed hard. There really wasn't anywhere for her to go if she stepped back. And darn it, she didn't want to step back.

"Um. Okay." She spun around quickly and pulled the plates out of the cupboard. "I'll dish it up, you can serve it. That work for you?" Her voice was a little too high and her hand a little too unsteady, so the plates rattled against each other as she set them down. Matt stepped back and she moved around him to grab the salad. She pulled out two bottles of salad dressing, ranch and Italian. "Which, if either, do you like?"

"Ranch is fine," he said. "Do the kids get any?"

"Eli does. Liam's not really a fan."

He chuckled and the sound hit her down low. Very, very low. Goodness.

She turned to the stove and managed to dish up the fragrant, gooey casserole without spilling any. Her handoffs to Matt were carefully managed so she didn't accidentally touch his hand. If he noticed she was being overly careful in her movements, he didn't let on.

"What would you like to drink?" she asked him as she turned to the fridge. "I don't really have any man drinks." She hadn't stopped to buy anything, either, thinking it would be too much. In fact, she'd done a great job of overthinking everything about what was supposed to be *just a friendly dinner.*

He arched a brow as she put the half gallon of chocolate milk on the counter. "Man drinks? I can't have chocolate milk, too?"

Her face burned. That had been a stupid way to put it. "Oh. Of course you can."

He moved in a little closer. "I'm just teasing," he said softly. "I'm sorry. Water is fine."

She busied herself with the drinks and was relieved when Matt left the kitchen. She gathered up the glasses and joined them at the table. Aldo, she noticed, had lain down underneath it. He didn't lift his head from his paws, but he did thump his tail.

Both boys were peering under the table.

She managed not to smile. "Guys. You need to eat, then you can play with Aldo. Okay?"

Matt jumped in. "He doesn't mind waiting. I fed him before we came over here." To Callie, he said, "This is great. I've only ever had mac and cheese from a box."

She laughed. "I'll make sure I tell my mom. It's her recipe. Usually if the kids have mac and cheese, it's from a box. But this version—" she stopped herself from saying *is for special occasions* and finished "—is for company."

Eli was not to be deterred by small talk. "We can't have a dog." This was accompanied by a sideways look at Callie. She took a bite of her mac and cheese to cover her smile.

Matt glanced at her casually. "Your dad wanted a dog when he was a kid, too."

Eli's eyes got huge. "He did? How do you know?"

Callie held her breath. This was what worried her, bringing Jason in so suddenly like this. Matt smiled at Eli. "We were neighbors when we were growing up, like you and I are now."

"Our dad died," Eli told him. "That means he's not here anymore, but he watches us from heaven."

Callie's throat tightened at the matter-of-fact delivery, and she saw a mirror of her own sorrow flash across Matt's face. "I know," he said and his voice was steady. "But he and I were best friends from the time we were your age, Eli."

Eli frowned. "You were a kid?"

Callie nearly choked on her mac and cheese, and she heard Matt's muffled laugh. "Of course he was, Eli," she gasped. "All grown-ups were kids once."

"You okay, Callie?" Matt asked, the sorrow in his gaze replaced by amusement.

"Fine," she managed to reply. She reached for her water glass. Kids and their impeccable timing.

Matt told them stories about their dad, about the dog he never did get, though not for lack of trying, and Callie was relieved Matt worded things in such a way as not to encourage them to take matters into their own hands. The last thing she needed was to have them decide to get a dog on their own, which was actually how the story of Jason wanting a dog had ended. His parents had made him return the puppy, and he'd ever afterward teased them that he was still traumatized from the incident, even as an adult.

When the main course was over, she brought

in the box of cookies and let them choose one beautifully decorated sugar cookie each. Matt had bought cookies in the shapes of trains and trucks, which were a hit, of course. When the kids went to wash up, she began to clear the table.

He helped her pick up the plates, but she shooed him out of the kitchen. "It'll only take me a few minutes to do this." Also, she was far less likely to drop something if he wasn't right there, taking up all the air in the room and making her nervous.

He put the plates in the sink. "All right. I'll go play with the boys, if that's okay."

"That's fine," she murmured, and tried not to focus on the rear view as he left the kitchen. She shut her eyes instead. Then opened them quickly when she realized how stupid she'd look, standing there with her eyes closed, if he turned and caught her.

Callie heard the rattling of the Lego bricks as the boys opened the cartons, and then the chatter of their voices and the lower tones of Matt's. While it was a happy sound, it still made her heart hurt. She braced her arms on the counter and let her head fall forward.

Tears blurred her vision for just a moment. Jason had never gotten the chance to play with Lego sets with his sons. They'd been far too little when he died. Liam hadn't been two yet. It should have been Jason in there—but it wasn't, and no amount of wishing would make it so.

She shrugged her shoulders and focused on cleaning the kitchen. It was sweet of Matt to make time for her boys. After all, they were an important link for him, too, to the friend he'd lost.

She went out there after she'd put the last plate in the dishwasher. Truthfully, she could have waited on cleaning up. It was a pretty simple meal. But it was a kind of buffer between her and these weird feelings she was experiencing toward Matt, and she needed to shore up her defenses again. Laughter—and a friendly bark—erupted from the living room, and she dried her hands on a towel before she went back out to see what was going on. She had to pause when she caught sight of them.

Both boys were piled on Matt, and he was laughing along with them. Aldo was in there, too, tongue lolling and tail going a mile a minute. Lego towers had collapsed and scattered—maybe due to the tail—and she thought there was a block under Matt's hip, but he never let on. The boys laughed gleefully, full-on belly laughs that made her smile even as her heart stuttered. She made herself walk in there, and hoped her pounding heart wasn't obvious to Matt.

"Wow, what are you guys doing to Mr. Bowden?" she teased, and he caught her eye with a wink. Her mouth actually went dry. If a man playing with her kids could make her all mushy inside—and it wasn't as if there weren't people to play with them—what did that mean? Why this man? Why now?

"We've got him, Mama!" Eli shrieked, and Liam laughed his big baby laugh. She opened her mouth to say something about indoor voices, but then closed it again.

"I see that. Don't hurt him, guys," she said instead, and they laughed harder. She sat on the couch and tucked her feet under her and watched the show, amusement warring with worry. This was not what she'd expected to happen. This was…bonding. Aldo came over and sat in front of her, his big head cocked to the side. She gave in and rubbed him between the ears, but couldn't quell the feeling that she needed to stop this. Now. Before it got any worse.

She clapped her hands to get their attention. "Okay, guys, pick up. Time to get ready for bed." She couldn't have bonding. That was bad. It meant they were becoming emotionally attached to Matt, which meant they could get hurt. Matt must have heard the slight edge of panic in her voice, because he looked up and caught both boys in a hug.

"You heard your mom. Let's get this cleaned up." Over the grumbles, they all picked up, then Callie directed them toward the bedrooms to collect their jammies and get ready for baths.

"Thanks for coming," she said, knowing she was being unspeakably rude to practically shove Matt out the door like this, but unable to stop herself. To his credit, he swiftly snagged his jacket, snapped on Aldo's leash and moved toward the door.

"Thanks so much for dinner, Callie," he said, and she couldn't meet his eyes.

"You're welcome," she managed to reply, and shut the door behind them. Then she could breathe again, once he wasn't taking up all the oxygen in the whole house. She rested her head on the door. Now she felt crappy for booting him out, but it had all been way too cozy for her peace of mind.

She couldn't risk it.

Matt walked home slowly. Callie's neighbor, who did day care in her home, was getting out of her car as he and Aldo came down the front steps. He returned her wave and didn't miss, even in the gathering darkness, the look of blatant speculation she sent toward Callie's house.

Callie wouldn't like that.

Not after what he'd seen in her eyes. Panic, pure and simple. Somehow he'd crossed a line and it had freaked her out. All evening she'd watched him carefully, clearly not comfortable with him in her house as he played with her kids. She'd been especially spooked when the currents between the two of them flowed hot. But she'd made the effort to be friendly for her children's sake, and for the sake of her husband's memory.

Matt kicked a stone as he walked up his own driveway. He'd like to chalk this evening up to a favor for a buddy's widow, but it was clearly more than that. He was attracted to her, and that was something he'd have to quash if he wanted to be around her and her boys. Clearly, the whole idea was unpalatable to her.

Aldo whined as Matt unlocked the door, and he rubbed the dog's head. "Want to go for a run?" he asked, and Aldo responded with the whole-body wiggle and a yelp. "All right. Let me change and we'll go."

One thing he'd always loved was night runs. It wasn't something he'd been able to do in Afghanistan. So he and Aldo headed out into the cool night. Chilly, but not raining or snowing. The sidewalks were mostly snow-free, because it had been warm enough to do some melting today. Pretty decent for late March in Michigan.

The streets were quiet enough, some traffic, but he wanted to avoid too much foot traffic. It made Aldo nervous, and Matt had made too much progress with the dog to undo it now. Not unlike Callie, he supposed. She was fighting her own personal war and there wasn't much he could do. He didn't know what Jason would want him to do. Watch out for them, sure. Make certain she was okay and maybe even happy. But Matt didn't think that was what Callie wanted. He wasn't sure what had spooked her tonight—though he could guess. He'd clicked with her kids.

Who did he honor? His longtime friend? Or the friend's widow, to whom he was attracted?

Matt shoved it all away and focused on the fall of his feet against the sidewalk, a familiar rhythm, and the way Aldo loped a little bit ahead, tongue lolling. His head blessedly emptied of all thoughts—but Callie and her panicked eyes were still there, in the back of his mind.

"So. I saw one superhunky neighbor leaving your house last night," Colleen teased the next morning, after the boys had disappeared into the day care part of the house. Callie felt her face turn bright red as her mouth dropped open. She hadn't actually planned for this, on top of a night spent tossing and turning, and full of dreams of Matt kissing her—*kissing her*, dear God. It hadn't occurred to her that someone would see him coming or going. And draw conclusions. That were completely wrong, of course.

"Um. Yeah," she said, her recovery slow and awkward, but still… "He just stopped in to see the boys. Since he knew Jason and all." She busied herself with backpacks, and wished the kids hadn't abandoned her so quickly.

Colleen made a noise in her throat that could have meant anything. "Okay."

"Colleen—" Callie started, but her friend stopped her, holding up a hand. "I know, Callie. I won't say anything. Well, that's not true," she amended, and Callie had to smile. "I'll say he seems like a great guy. And I know you could use a great guy in your life."

Callie's smile faded. "No. We're fine just how we are."

Colleen didn't push it, but her look said volumes. "Are you?"

Of course they were. She'd worked very hard to be sure they were. It was her main priority. A great guy in her life? Other than her boys, that wasn't on the list.

That evening, a respectable amount of time after Matt pulled into the driveway, Callie trekked over to his house. She knocked, half hoping he wouldn't answer. He tugged open the door a few seconds later, disheveled and sweaty in a T-shirt and gym shorts that showed off—oh, my—powerful thighs. She wanted—inexplicably—to lick him all over.

Not helpful.

"Can I help you?" he asked, sounding slightly amused, and she realized she'd been staring. There was no hiding the resulting heat that swept up her neck.

She cleared her throat. Her voice seemed to be stuck. "Did I interrupt something?"

"Not really. I just finished my workout."

"Ah." Her mind blanked at the thought of him lifting weights. Muscles flexing. *Mmm...*

"Callie?" Now he sounded really amused.

She blinked. "Right. Sorry. Been a long day. Listen, I just wanted to apologize for my rudeness last night," she said, and made herself meet those amazing blue eyes. Here was the tricky part. She didn't want to admit how badly she'd freaked out. "It just got a little—overwhelming."

"I know." He leaned on the door.

"You know?" she repeated. Her stomach dropped. She'd hoped she'd been a little more subtle. Apparently not.

"Yeah. I could tell. Where are the kids?"

She glanced over her shoulder. "In the house. Standing in the doorway so they can see me." Matt looked around her and waved, and they waved back at him excitedly. What did he mean, he could tell? How could he read her? He didn't know her, not really. "I'm really sorry. I never should have run you out of the house like I did last night." It still made her wince, that she'd gotten so panicky over them playing. *Bonding.*

"Callie. It's okay," he said softly, and she gave a stiff nod.

"Okay. Just wanted to make sure."

He caught her arm as she turned, and lightly pulled her around. The heat of his touch, gentle as it was, made her shiver.

"I could tell," he repeated, his voice slightly rough, "because you looked completely spooked. Not unlike Aldo during a thunderstorm."

She thought maybe she should be offended, even as, behind him, Aldo raised his head and wagged his tail at the sound of his name. "I'm not—"

"No. You're not. You're trying to deal with all this and it got to be too much. No shame in that. You've been through hell, Callie. I know that." Matt released her arm when she gave a slight tug. The last thing she needed was for Colleen or any other neighbor to look outside and see them… well, see them together, period. "I know that and I know this is a weird situation. So we'll take it at your pace. I'd love to hang out with your kids. But if it's too much, and you need to step back, I get it." He ran his hand over his closely cropped hair. "Jason was important to me, but you were his wife. That means my access to your kids is up to you."

She stepped back. He was giving her the control here and she appreciated it. "Glad you understand that. And again, I'm sorry."

He smiled, but it didn't reach his eyes, which were understandably wary. "No problem. It was a great dinner. And I enjoyed the company. So did Aldo."

This time the dog gave a little bark at the sound of his name. She couldn't help but smile a little.

"That's good. Well, I'll let you get back to your workout."

"Okay."

She walked back across the street and felt his gaze on her the whole way. She kept her steps measured, even though she wanted to run, because she really didn't want him to *know* she wanted to run. And hide. And ignore him until these feelings went so far away they never came back.

CHAPTER FIVE

THE BOYS WERE wiggling at the front door when she walked back up to her own house.

"Can we see Aldo?" Eli demanded, and Callie made herself smile.

"Not today, kiddo." Goodness, all this fuss over a dog. She ushered them back a bit so she could step in, and didn't look over her shoulder. What if Matt was watching? What if he wasn't? Both options gave her a little flutter, which she tried to ignore.

It was silly either way.

Her phone rang as she was steering the boys toward bedtime. A quick glance revealed it to be her mother-in-law.

"Hi, Maureen." She tucked the phone on her shoulder and pulled jammies out for Liam.

"Hi, Callie," Maureen Marshall said. "Listen, Joe and I were wondering if we could take the boys this weekend. Overnight on Saturday, to be exact. We can get tickets to the Sesame Street Live show and thought maybe they'd enjoy that. I know it's kind of short notice, but…" She trailed off.

Callie smiled at Liam and tweaked his nose as she handed him the jammies and stepped back to let him try to put them on. "It's fine. I think they'd like it." And maybe she could pick up a shift at the salon Saturday morning. The extra money would be useful.

"Okay, good. Thanks, Callie. Do you have to work? We can pick them up beforehand."

"No, but I'll see if I can get a shift," she replied as she helped Liam yank the pajama top over his head. He had a really big head and she liked to say it was because he had a big—and very smart—brain.

They settled on a time. She'd offered to meet them somewhere, but Maureen insisted on making the full trip over to them. It wasn't a long drive, but it saved Callie half an hour or so of her morning.

"Guess what?" she told the kids after she hung

up. "You can go to Grandma and Grandpa's this weekend. Would you like that?"

Their excited squeals made her laugh. She hugged each boy in turn and said, "It's still a few days away. But it will be fun to look forward to."

"So, tomorrow?" Eli asked, and she dropped a kiss on his head and chuckled.

"Nope. Saturday. Today's Wednesday, so two more days." She pulled the covers back on each boy's bed.

She got them tucked in and went through all the rituals. She knew they were just stalling, even with Liam's eyes barely open, but she couldn't help but play along. They wouldn't be little for long. All too soon they'd be too big for her to tuck in. She would put that moment off for as long as possible.

Lori's eyes lit up the next morning when Callie asked about working on Saturday. "As it turns out, yes, I could definitely use you. Dawn can't make it and we've got that wedding to do. So if you can take Dawn's place, that saves me from having to reschedule her clients." Lori studied the book. They inputted appointments and schedules into the computer, too, but she preferred the paper schedule for a quick glance.

"I can," Callie confirmed, and Lori penciled her in. Callie would be here in plenty of time for the nine-thirty appointment. And she'd be done at noon or so. Which actually gave her pretty much the whole day to do—what? She didn't think about it too much. Just decided she'd get a jump start on yard work and spring cleaning. Not a bad way to spend a kid-free day.

"Excellent. On another note," Lori said, "Sharon called in this morning, so it's just you and me. Her daughter is sick again." Her boss tapped her pencil on the book. "I'm trying to reschedule whatever doesn't fit into our schedules."

"That's fine," Callie said, and Lori turned the book so Callie could see it. She noted her nearly full schedule. Her heart sank just a little at the very last appointment of the day—a color. It'd take awhile, which meant she'd pick the boys up later than usual. "Looks good. I'll call Colleen and let her know I'll be a little late."

Lori put her finger on the color appointment.

"Are you sure? I can reschedule it. I know it's late for you. I've got one at the same time or I'd take it."

Callie shook her head and smiled. "It's fine. Eli and Liam love being at Colleen's. They won't even notice if I'm late." She meant it as a joke, but unfortunately the words fell into the "sad but true" category.

Lori slipped an arm around her shoulders and gave her a squeeze. "Oh, I think they'll notice. They love you and they know how much you love them. But you're right, they'll be okay."

Lori had been a rock for Callie through the dark days. She'd been there, held the job open for her until she emerged from the fog of grief enough to be able to function in the real world. She'd called her and brought her food once a week, and made sure she ate otherwise. Callie owed her a lot more than staying a little late to pick up some slack.

"You're a great friend," Callie said, even though the words were inadequate.

Lori just laughed. "You'd do the same for me," she said with a wave of a slim hand.

I hope I never have to. But Callie didn't say the words—just smiled, because it was true.

The day moved along pretty quickly, and Callie was grateful to get off her feet at the end of it. Her color appointment had run over—which she'd expected—and it made her even later. The boys were happy to see her, but dinner was going to be a rush affair if she wanted to avoid the breakdowns and tears from overly hungry kids. Seeing how quickly they were approaching the critical point, she called The Pie Shack and ordered a pizza. The wait wasn't bad, since it was a weeknight. Plus they'd deliver.

Not a great mom day, she thought as she shoveled laundry into the washer. But you couldn't win them all. And Callie was smart enough not to try.

The bell rang for the pizza and she opened the front door to pay the delivery guy—but it was Matt on her step, holding her steaming and fragrant pizza box. She blinked and took a step back. "Whoa. I thought—wait. You're the delivery boy?"

He flashed her a wicked smile that had her face immediately heating. "Only for you."

Flustered, she reached for her wallet. "Well. Okay—"

"I got it, Callie. I caught the kid in the driveway. It's all set."

She turned around, her wallet clutched tightly in her hands. "Oh, no. I can't do that. Let me pay you—" But the boys came tumbling in then, asking about Aldo, and her words were lost. She stepped aside with a little sigh. "You may as well come in."

He stepped in and two little boys attached themselves to his legs. He handed the pizza to her with a smile and she carried it to the table, not wanting to see him roughhousing with the kids. When would she get used to it?

She got plates out in the kitchen and took a moment. Maybe she needed to relax a little. Not read anything into it or fight this and it'd just go away on its own. Understandable that she might overreact the first time she was attracted to a man. It'd been so long.

He came into the kitchen then, Eli and Liam in tow.

"Are you staying?" she asked him, in a voice that was just a little too bright.

He shook his head. "No, I don't want to impose."

"Please stay," Eli implored, and Liam smiled his big baby grin. "Pizza is yummy."

"Ah." Matt threw a helpless glance Callie's way. "Yes, it is."

She gave in. "Do you have any other plans? If not, you're welcome to stay." She nearly swallowed her tongue. What had made her issue the invitation? Just good manners, or something more?

Just good manners, surely. After all, he'd paid for the pizza.

But as he accepted the plate she held out, she knew it was more than that. The kids lit up when he was around and they didn't do that often. So she would swallow her awkwardness and let him visit occasionally with the boys like this. She'd adjust.

"So, Matt, why did you come back here to

live?" Callie asked when the boys cleared out post pizza, leaving the two of them alone. It seemed like a pretty safe conversational topic.

He paused. "Brice and Marley made me an offer," he said finally. "They knew I'd been looking at doing something like this, once I—once I retired." The tightness of his jaw indicated maybe retiring hadn't been his first choice.

"Why did you retire? Jason always said you were well suited to the army." She was genuinely curious.

Matt didn't meet her gaze for a minute. "It was time," he said finally. "I'd just seen too much. Kind of catches up to you after a while."

"I understand." She knew all about sore spots being prodded, and would leave his be. She changed the subject instead. "So, what is it you guys do?"

She saw him relax. "It's an adventure company. Out There Adventures. We do things like whitewater rafting, mountain biking, all over the Midwest. We meet the tour at the site." He'd lit right up as he talked about it, even as her heart sank. Then she felt—what, exactly? It couldn't be disappointment, could it? No, it had to be a feeling of relief. This was what she wanted, right? A concrete reason to avoid him. To shore up her defenses when she got those—feelings.

Even if she'd ever been interested in him, she wasn't going to get involved with a guy who took those kinds of risks with his life on a regular basis. Period.

"Problem?" Matt's voice cut through her thoughts.

She refocused. "Oh, no. Not at all. I was just thinking it's kind of cool you and your friends could start a company like that." It was true. She did think that, even if it was all wrong for her and her family. "There's a lot of risk involved."

He misunderstood what she meant by risk, and she let it stand. "Yeah, but there is in starting any business. We talked about it and researched it for a long time. Well, I did what I could from Afghanistan and they did a lot here." He shrugged. "Time will tell if it will pay off. But we're booking tours hand over fist and that's a good sign."

"Yes," she agreed. "It is. So you'll be gone a lot?"

He reached down to grab a stray toy truck and

she tried not to notice the way his shirt pulled across his chest. She averted her eyes and rubbed at a crayon mark on the table instead. Goodness. "We'll trade off. But yes, it will mostly be a few days at a time. We've got four other guides, so we'll rotate. That way no one has to be gone for several consecutive trips." He gave a short laugh. "Unless they want to be, of course."

"That sounds very sensible," she murmured. Was it good or bad to have him gone for periods at a time? She wouldn't have to worry about running into him accidentally. That was a bonus. Right?

He flashed the grin that did disturbing things to her insides. "Yeah. I'm pretty stoked about it. It's a great fit. I'm not an office kind of guy. After twenty years in the army I'm not sure I could transition to a desk job."

Liam came up to her then with two big Lego blocks that were stuck together. As she worked them apart she asked, "What happened with your fiancée?" Horror shot through her. "Oh. I'm so sorry. That was awfully rude. Forget I said anything."

He chuckled, which she didn't expect. "No harm done, Callie. It just didn't work out. Better all around."

Callie wanted to ask him exactly what he meant by that, but she understood the nonanswer. After all, she'd given plenty of her own over the past year and a half. "I'm sorry."

He shrugged. "These things happen."

He didn't seem particularly broken up about it, but there was a definite shadow in his eyes. Maybe he wasn't completely over his ex, after all. It was another reason this attraction to him was a bad idea. A hopeless cause was another kind of risk entirely.

"Well." She stood and picked up her plate. "Good luck with your new venture. I hope it takes off for you. But don't—please don't say anything about all your extreme sports to the kids. I'm trying to keep that sort of thing off their radar." She planned to keep them as far from anything that could hurt them as possible.

Matt didn't say anything, but her comment rocked him. She was afraid of something happening to her kids. He got that. But she couldn't hide them from life forever. He knew all about wanting to protect someone. Thing was, people had a way of making choices and decisions on their own. Like walking into places where the threat of death was a constant companion. But who was he to point that out to her? This friendship was still pretty tenuous and he really didn't want to spoil it now by falling out with her.

He followed her into the small kitchen and found her bent over, rearranging things to fit the pizza box in the fridge. The view was fantastic—and wrong—so he forced himself to look over her head at the milk carton as he grabbed the door, which was swinging slowly back toward her.

"Will it fit?"

She stood up and spun around, and he saw the second she realized she was trapped between him and the fridge. He didn't move. He couldn't. He was caught in the caramel depths of her eyes. He definitely saw a spark of what burned in him reflected there. If he leaned in just a little bit he could take her mouth. Just. A. Little. Bit. Closer.

Her intake of breath was audible and her hand

visibly shook when she put it on his chest. "Matt. I'm not—I can't—"

He stepped back, when what he wanted to do was step forward and pull her in, kiss her until the shadows fled from her caramel-colored eyes and she only saw him. The light caught the diamond on her finger. The icy flash was as good as a cold blast of water to the face. He reached out and touched the rings and saw her eyes go wide. There was nothing more to say.

As long as those rings were on her finger, there'd always be a third party between them. He had no say in that, and he respected it, and what they represented. She would move on in her own time—or not. He also realized he was all wrong for her. She deserved someone who could give her everything. All of himself. He wasn't that guy. He'd been alone for too long, as his foray into the world of the almost-married had proved. He could handle a dog, not a ready-made family. "I know. I know you can't." He fisted his hand so he wouldn't be tempted to reach out and touch her face. Wrong for her or not, he still wanted to touch her, chase the shadows from her eyes.

It was time to go.

He moved away as she turned and fiddled with something in the fridge. He stepped back even farther, recognizing her nervousness and wanting to give her the space she needed.

He swallowed as the kids came back in. He said his goodbyes to her and those cute boys of hers, and walked back across the street to his dog. He couldn't resist turning to look back at her house, all brightly lit and warm and inviting.

He could see her silhouetted against the door. She gave him a quick little wave and shut it, and he started walking again.

It was really too bad neither of them was in a place to pursue this mutual attraction. But he knew he should just stick with Aldo. A dog wasn't complicated. No game playing, unless you counted fetch. Loyal. No backstabbing. You knew where you stood with a dog, unlike with some people.

Matt flicked on the kitchen light and headed for the dining room table, stopping to rub Aldo behind the ears. Time for paperwork. It didn't keep Matt warm at night, but at least it didn't twist him up in those stupid knots, unlike Callie's haunting caramel eyes.

Callie released a breath she hadn't known she was holding after Matt left. She'd watched him walk across the street. It was silly but she couldn't seem to pull her eyes off him. He took up so much space and made it so hard for her to act normally. She wanted to burrow into that broad chest—except at the same time she didn't. She fiddled with her rings. She wore them as a shield; she knew that perfectly well. They deterred men, but not, apparently, herself from noticing Matt. Ironic.

She never thought she'd need to protect herself from, well, herself. She'd had everything under such tight control, she'd never expected to have issues like being attracted to another man. That another man might do for her what Jason had. And that said man would be a friend of Jason's.

Wasn't that a betrayal of her marriage somehow?

Callie turned back toward the living room. That was silly and she knew it. She'd even been to counseling, where the woman told her it wasn't any such thing. Jason had been gone more than a year. Closer to two, really. He would never expect her to spend her life alone. But Callie had accepted it. That she'd raise their kids and then sort of see where she was when they left home.

Nice and vague.

But her mom had made an equally valid point the other day—that the boys would try to take responsibility for Callie at too young an age, and she didn't want that, either.

She went in her room to grab more laundry, and sat down on her big bed for a minute. Oh, she didn't really want to be alone for years and years on end. No one did. Raising two rambunctious kids was going to be tough by herself. But if she did look for a man it wouldn't be a guy who ran an adventure company and did dangerous stuff like white-water rafting for a living.

And never mind she'd once loved that same kind of sport. In fact, it was how she'd met Jason—on a white-water rafting trip. She knew all about the risks he was taking. Had embraced them once, even.

She couldn't take them anymore. Not after Jason's death.

Sure, Matt also did kind things like play with the kids. Buy her pizza. Shovel her driveway. And apparently, take in strays like Aldo—from Afghanistan.

Make her feel all fizzy inside.

Callie tipped over onto her pillow and let out a frustrated roar. All tied up in knots over a man and she hadn't even seen it coming. If that darn dog had just stayed in the right yard, she wouldn't be in this situation. She rolled over on her back and stared at the ceiling. Eventually they'd have run into each other. He lived across the street from her. It was inevitable.

"You okay, Mama?" Eli's voice startled her from her ridiculous musings.

She sat up and smiled at him, holding out her arms for a hug. "I am. Thanks, honey." As she drew her little boy in, she closed her eyes tight, wishing she could just shut the rest of the world out.

The next day, Matt kept his thoughts off Callie, but it took far more effort than it should have.

His day was busy, but she still crept into his head when he didn't expect it.

"There's a word my grandma used to use," Marley said conversationally. "Woolgathering. For moments like right now, when it's clear the person you're talking to is off someplace far, far away, mentally."

Caught. Matt winced. "Sorry, Marley. I've just got—a lot on my mind."

"Of course you do," she agreed. "But you're not a woolgatherer. So it's a woman, right? Your neighbor, Callie?"

He was not discussing Callie with Marley. "I'm just tired and busy." Both true, but Marley was spot-on with her assessment. Far too much so, in fact. So he'd be more careful not to wander off mentally and give himself away. But he still couldn't seem to put Callie too far out of his mind.

"Well, the next step is mooning over her." She gave him a smug little smile. "I give you a week."

Matt tipped his chair back. "You're pretty funny." There was no way he'd moon over a woman. Ever. He'd never even gotten moony over Trina, and he'd been planning to marry her. Of course, she hadn't been the type you got that way over. She wouldn't have liked it.

Neither would Callie. He dropped the chair back down. The last thing he wanted to do was scare her away. Not for his sake, but for what he hoped he could share with her boys. Jason's boys.

Yeah, Jason was really the focus here. Or should be.

Marley snapped her fingers in front of his face. "There you go again. Boom, you're gone. Is there something going on with Callie, Matt?"

Annoyed, he rubbed his hands over his face. He couldn't deny anything, which annoyed him further. "Marley. Drop it. Please."

She sighed. "Why does it have to be a bad thing?" Before he could answer, she held up her hands. "But okay. Consider it dropped."

"What's dropped?" Brice stepped up behind his wife and kissed her neck.

She reached behind her to pat his face. "The subject of Matt's new woman, honey."

Matt groaned. Brice lifted his head and met Matt's eyes, his own full of humor. "Ah. I see. Who's the woman, Matt? Callie?"

Hell. "No one. No woman." Matt ground his teeth together as he stood up and moved around them.

"Definitely Callie," he heard Marley say triumphantly. "Nothing else would make him so touchy."

"Leave him alone, Mar," came Brice's amused reply.

Matt went into his office and resisted the far-too-teenage urge to slam the door. Great. Just great. Marley was on the trail now and it'd be hell to get her off it. And Brice would let her pick at him, unless Matt said something. And then he'd get knowing looks from Brice, too. But it was still probably worth the trade-off.

So he'd say something and hope his friend called his wife off the scent. Or maybe if he introduced Marley to Callie, she'd see there was nothing between them.

But that was kind of playing right into her hands, wasn't it?

CHAPTER SIX

CALLIE DIDN'T SEE Matt for the rest of the week. She caught glimpses of lights on in the house or saw his truck in the driveway, but Aldo didn't show up once on her porch.

She told herself she was relieved, not disappointed. At all.

If she kept thinking it, it would be true. Right?

Either way, she was packing for her kids' overnight stay with Grandma and Grandpa tomorrow. Miracle of miracles, she'd gotten all the laundry done, so she could cross that off her weekend list.

The TV in the living room was tuned to the evening news and the meteorologist was talking about some storms that were coming in off Lake Michigan. Not snow this time, but wind and rain. Very likely severe in nature.

Callie sighed as she dropped clean undies in Eli's bag. Of course they would be. She hated storms, and knew how bad they could be here in the spring, but tried very hard to hide it from her kids.

The day had been unseasonably warm—hence the coming storms—and Callie had left the front door open. She heard a scratching and a whine and realized her earlier thoughts about Aldo had been too soon. Hoping the kids wouldn't notice him, she hurried to the door, but then the dog started barking, bringing out the boys.

"Doggie," Liam cried, and Callie bit back a sigh.

"Yep. There he is." She put her hands on her hips and stared down into Aldo's upturned face. He was watching her intently. She rubbed his head and he gave another bark, a sharp one, his eyes not leaving her. She snatched her hand back, but his tail was wagging.

"We take him home, Mama?" Eli asked, and Callie nodded. There was something off with the dog today. Maybe he didn't like the coming weather, either. She looked across the street. The truck was in the driveway.

"Yep, we need to get him home. Let's go before it rains." The kids shoved their feet into their boots and they all trekked across the street, only to meet Matt coming out.

"Sorry, Callie. Darn it, I thought I'd gotten the problem fixed." He reached for Aldo's collar and his fingers brushed hers. She couldn't let go of the collar, as she felt the dog quivering under her hand, but more than that felt the heat from Matt's touch—and it wasn't even intentional.

Thunder rumbled in the distance and Aldo hit the ground on his belly, whining. Callie let go, startled. Eli and Liam looked at Matt with huge eyes. "Doggie scared," said Liam, and Matt nodded.

"He is. Loud noises scare him. It's left over from where he lived before. I'm going to get him inside, where he feels safer."

"I don't like thunder, either," said Eli solemnly, and Callie caught Matt's gaze.

"Lots of people don't like thunder," he said calmly, and smiled at the boy. "You aren't the only one."

Callie glanced at the sky, which was the purple of a particularly violent bruise. She understood what Aldo was feeling. Her own anxiety was rising. But she forced her voice to be calm. "Well, we'll head back in. Maybe put on a movie." She started to turn the boys in that direction, and Aldo barked again.

"Why not come to my place?" The words were out before Matt could stop them. It was actually supposed to be a severe storm, so having them in his house meant he wouldn't worry about them. He wasn't responsible for them, he knew that. But they were beginning to be important to him.

"Can we, Mom? Can we?" Both boys turned their considerable charm on their mother, who gave Matt an exasperated look. He should have asked her first, out of their earshot.

Thunder rumbled again and Aldo whimpered harder. Callie looked up again as the wind gusted harder. "Okay," she said, though reluctance was clear in her voice. "I'm going to grab a couple things. We'll be over in five."

He glanced at the sky. They wouldn't have much longer than that. Aldo's reaction told him this wasn't going to be a run-of-the-mill storm. "Leave them with me. But Callie? Hurry."

"Boys, go with Matt." She met his gaze and he knew how hard it was for her to let them go. "I'll be right back."

He turned the boys and the dog toward his house, and she dashed off toward her own home. Aldo let out a howl that made him shiver.

The boys' eyes were still huge. Matt smiled at them, hoping to reassure them. "He's okay, guys. Just doesn't like storms. He'll be okay. How about a snack?"

"Okay," Eli said, looking a little more heartened, and Liam nodded, too.

Aldo took off for Matt's room, where Matt knew he'd settle in under the bed.

He'd left the TV on and the weather guy was talking. Not wanting to scare them, Matt grabbed the remote and muted it, then herded them into the kitchen. He didn't have much in the way of snacks, but maybe he had some crackers or something else kid-friendly. He pulled open the fridge. A carton of milk, a few beers. Eggs. Cheese. Takeout containers. He pulled out the cheese and pushed the door shut. Doubtful anything else in there was edible. Callie wouldn't be happy if he gave the kids food poisoning.

What was she thinking? Callie rummaged around, unplugged her computer, flipped on a couple lights so they wouldn't come home to a dark house. Aldo's reaction had unnerved her. She didn't like storms herself. Never had. Jason used to laugh at her, but he'd been only too happy to distract her from her fear in the sweetest of ways.

Obviously Matt wasn't going to do that.

Refocusing, she tossed a few extra things into the diaper bag they didn't really need anymore, but which still came in handy. Snacks, a couple movies so the kids could choose, a sippy cup for Liam. Her phone, charger, her keys. A book, so she could pretend to be detached. Glow sticks just in case the power went out. Heaven forbid.

By the time she was on her front porch, locking the door, the wind had kicked up and the rain was starting. She raced across the street and found Matt waiting for her, the door open.

"Just in time," he observed, closing it behind

her. The thunder crashed, earning shrieks—not entirely of fear—from the kitchen, and Callie jumped.

She saw the concern on his face, and she felt her own heat in response. It was a silly thing, to be afraid of storms as an adult. He said nothing, though, and she turned away to rummage in the bag for the movies. "Is it okay if they watch these?"

"Of course." He led the way into the living room. Callie toed off her shoes and followed him. He lowered his voice. "We'll need to keep an eye out though, Callie. Some of these weather warnings look bad."

"Oh." She stared at the radar on the muted screen, at the angry swirl of reds and yellows rolling off Lake Michigan. That looked worse than "bad."

He changed the channel to the video setting. "I've got another TV in the kitchen, and my laptop is charged. So we'll use those to keep an eye on the weather. Don't want to freak out the kids."

She was touched by his thoughtfulness. "Right. Of course not. Thank you."

The kids came into the living room and wrapped themselves around her. She held them, tamping down her own dislike of turbulent weather so they wouldn't pick up on it. Storms tended to be violent in the spring. Not always resulting in things like tornadoes, but high winds, hail and lots of noise. Messy.

"Let's get this started," she said as cheerfully as she could manage. "Which one?"

The kids picked a Bob the Builder movie and Matt got it going. The boys settled on the couch with their special blankets that she'd grabbed, hoping they'd help keep the kids calm.

Matt met Callie in the kitchen. It was a guy kitchen, she thought, momentarily distracted by the huge coffee machine. He followed her gaze and gave a small smile.

"Good coffee was at a premium in my unit," he said. "Now that I'm out, it's one of those things I make sure I always have on hand."

"Makes sense," she agreed, and scanned the rest of the room.

The counters were bare except for a TV and toaster, and his laptop was open. There were cracker crumbs on the counter, where the boys must have been sitting. Her own counters were cluttered with canisters, kid stuff, paper, a few other appliances. She wasn't sure how Matt did it. Of course, when you lived alone, there was far less stuff. Especially if, as he claimed, he didn't cook.

He turned the TV on low as the wind picked up outside. She moved to the window to see tree branches whipping around and rain falling in sheets. It was dark enough that the streetlights had clicked on, even though it was still fairly early.

"Where's Aldo?" she asked, suddenly realizing she hadn't seen him since she'd come in.

"Under my bed," Matt answered. "I check on him occasionally, but he won't come out until it's over."

Callie understood completely. There were times she'd like to crawl under the bed and not come out. She felt a twinge of empathy for the embattled dog.

The weatherman talked on, showing places where hail was likely. Callie could hear it, hitting the roof and the porch. Matt gestured to her and she came over to see it layering the deck and yard in an icy mess. "Dime-size," he murmured. "Big enough to do quite a bit of damage."

The lights flickered and a cry went up from the living room. Callie hurried in there. Losing power was not on her list of favorite things to do with kids. They looked at her with big eyes and she sat on the couch between them and pulled them into her arms. They snuggled in and Callie forced her breathing to be level and even.

The power flickered again, then went out just as a huge crack sounded across the street. Callie jumped a mile, the kids screamed and Matt was in the room before she could even get to her feet.

"What was that?" She couldn't keep the wobble of fear out of her voice. It was dark in here, too dark. "Where's the bag? Guys, calm down, it's okay. I've got glow sticks."

"I think it's in the kitchen. Hold on." Thunder cracked again and she sat back down. Both kids immediately tried to climb into her lap, whimpering.

Matt was back in just a minute with a flashlight and the bag. She took both and, even with the kids on her lap, rummaged for the glow sticks she'd thrown in. She bent them to start them glowing and handed one to each boy. The bright sticks distracted them enough so they got off her lap, but sat close to her still. She slipped her arms around their shoulders and hugged them. "It's an adventure, guys. And it's almost over." She hoped.

"Callie." Matt was behind her, his tone grim. She looked up, and he pointed at the kids and shook his head.

"I've got to get up, guys." She kissed each one on the head with a calm she didn't feel, and walked over to Matt, the flashlight shaking in her hand.

He caught her hand and held it tight as he led her to the door. She let him, because he was scaring her. "Look."

She gasped when she followed his pointing finger. The tree in her front yard had come crashing down and her house was hidden behind the massive branches. Matt grabbed her when she reached for the door handle with a half sob.

"You can't go over there," he said. "Not yet. Not in the lightning. Look at the tree."

He was right, of course. In the flashes, she could see it had split clean in half, a sure sign it had been hit by lightning. Tears welled up and the flashlight fell to the floor as she pressed both hands to her mouth.

"My house. Matt! My house," she whispered, panic, fear and a kind of sickness welling up in her in one nauseating brew. She shook so badly that she didn't protest when he wrapped his arms around her and pulled her to his chest. She didn't know if she could have stayed upright on her own. She burrowed in, gripping handfuls of his shirt, trying to stay under control, feeling his heartbeat under her cheek. *Breathe.*

"I don't want the boys to see this," she whispered, and Matt stroked her hair and down her spine, then back up. Behind them, the kids were doing some sort of mock saber battle with the glow sticks. Thank God they were distracted.

Even in her panicky state, it felt good to lean on someone. Just for a few minutes. To draw strength from another person. This was what she'd missed so much about being married.

"You can stay here tonight," he said simply. "There's room. I've got an extra bedroom, and sleeping bags for the kids. You can have my room and I'll sleep on the couch. We'll go look at the mess as soon the storm stops enough that it's safe to go outside."

She took a deep breath and let it out in a shuddering exhalation. She stepped back, but Matt kept his arms around her loosely. She couldn't make herself pull away and break the connection that she desperately needed. He was right. Depending on where the tree had landed, there was a chance her house wasn't even habitable. "Okay. We'll stay here." A thought struck her and she turned to look again. "Matt. Is it on Colleen's, too?" She knew her neighbor wasn't home. She and her family had left on a vacation a few hours ago.

"I don't think so. It's hard to tell from this angle, though."

Callie pulled away this time and he let her go, his hands grazing her hips as she moved away.

She turned to look back at the broken tree, and squeezed her eyes shut tight, trying to stop a new flood of tears from breaking free. Crying would get her absolutely nowhere. She refocused on the issue at hand.

There was a change of clothes for both boys in the bag. Hopefully, a nighttime diaper for Liam, too. But nothing for her.

Though clearly, she couldn't go home yet.

"Thanks for letting us stay," she said, and her voice shook only a little.

Matt squeezed her shoulders, then let go. "You're welcome. I'll go check as soon as the lightning lets up."

She thought of the rain pouring into her little house, if there were holes. Tears pricked her eyes and she tried very hard to keep them in. She didn't want the boys to see her cry, and get worried.

Matt lifted her chin with a finger and that was all it took. "Oh, Callie. Come here." He pulled her in and she leaned on his solid chest, taking in his scent, once again feeling the steady beat of his heart under her cheek. It'd been so long since she'd just—just been held. She couldn't stop the seep of tears, but managed to swallow back any embarrassing sobs. She trembled from the effort and his arms tightened around her.

He was a total heel.

Here Callie was, all upset and emotional and worried, and he had her in his arms and was responding to her in the most inappropriate way.

It wasn't okay at any point. But now, when she was so upset? That made it worse. He tried not to think of her, not to breathe in her scent, not to notice the crush of her breasts against his chest. Again.

She stepped back and he let her go, far too reluctantly. "It'll be okay," he said. "We'll get through tonight and deal with the whole thing in the morning."

She sniffled a little, swiped her eyes and almost smiled. "Gosh. Sorry for all the waterworks." She took a shuddering breath.

"You've got reason," he said simply.

"Boys," she said as she went back over to them. "We're going to stay here tonight. Since we're already here." Her tone was mostly light and both kids cheered.

"Can we sleep with Aldo?" Eli asked, and Matt saw Callie shake her head.

"I don't know about that," she said. "We are guests and Aldo belongs to Matt."

"When he comes out, he might come find you," Matt said. "But it takes him a bit to settle down after a storm."

"It's dark," whimpered Liam, and Callie lifted him in her arms.

"It is," she agreed. "But you guys have your glow sticks. These big ones will stay lit all night. We'll put one in the bathroom, too, if that's okay?" She turned to face Matt.

"Of course," he said. Candles obviously wouldn't be a good plan with little kids, though he'd light some for the kitchen counter and other places that were elevated and out of the reach of little hands. He gave her major props for thinking of the glow sticks.

"Prepared for anything?" he asked, nodding at the package of them she'd fished out of the seemingly bottomless bag. She gave him a sheepish little smile.

"Yeah. I learned a while ago that these work well in the dark. Enough light they can see, but not so much they'll stay awake. And the novelty is a distraction. So I keep them on hand for things like this."

She clearly thought everything through. Planned for all eventualities. But from the shell-shocked look he could see in her eyes, he knew the disaster with the tree had thrown her way off. If there was one thing he was learning about Callie, it was that she was afraid to let things get out of her control.

"The rain is letting up," he noted. The time between the thunder and the lightning strikes was increasing, indicating the storm was moving off. He'd be able to go check the situation soon. If there was roof damage, he had a couple tarps, assuming the tree hadn't gone all the way through.

"Did you hear that?" she asked Eli and Liam. "It's letting up. And it's almost bedtime. Let's get that going, shall we?"

The kids were cheered by no baths, and Callie was clearly not happy with no toothbrushes. Matt rolled out the sleeping bags on the floor of the bedroom he was using as a weight room, and took two pillows off his bed. Then he stepped back as she tucked them in, with the stuffed animals they'd brought and a glow stick within reach of each boy. She joined him at the door and gave him a wan little smile.

"They're pretty worn out from all the excitement. I think they'll drop off pretty quickly, if Mother Nature cooperates."

"All right." He could see the squirmy little bundles on the floor and doubted they'd be out anytime soon, but what did he know? He wasn't a dad. His experience with kids was little to none. "I'm going to go look. Do you want to come, or want me to go check first?"

She closed her eyes, then opened them. "I'm going with you." Then her eyes went wide. "Oh, no! I completely forgot. My in-laws are collecting the kids first thing tomorrow. I'd better call them. Do you think they can get down the street?" She ran back to the bag and dug around until she pulled out her phone.

"Let's go see. It's still raining a bit." He took a windbreaker out of his hall closet and handed it to her. "Be a little big," he noted as she slipped it on. It hit her at the knee, and in spite of himself he grinned. "Nice look."

She rolled the sleeves up. "I bet. Thanks. Let's go."

Hail crunched under their feet as they walked up to the sidewalk. Now Matt could see the power line under the tree. He grabbed her hand. "Watch out. That's live."

She followed his gaze and her eyes widened. "Does that mean we can't get over there?"

He shook his head. "Not until the power company arrives."

There were branches down, but other than Callie's tree, the street looked passable. She called her in-laws and Matt stepped away to study the damage.

A few minutes later she came back over to him. "They'll be here tomorrow morning." She gestured at the tree across her driveway. "Since I won't be getting my van out."

"Nope."

He caught the sideways look she sent him. "Any chance I can get in there and get their weekend bags? They are all packed. The bedrooms are in the back."

He shook his head. "Not until that wire's taken care of."

She sighed. "All right. Hopefully, the power company will be here soon. Maureen and Joe have extra stuff for them, anyway. But there's other things they like to have with them...." Her voice trailed off and he took her hand. Her fingers were cold in his, even though it wasn't really that chilly out. She didn't seem to notice as she continued.

"I told my in-laws we were staying with you. They didn't know you were back." Her tone was almost absent as she stared at the tree. The smell of singed wood still filled the air. "Why didn't you tell them?"

He sighed. He hadn't been sure what to say. "I was going to look them up, too," he said. "But I guess I'll get a chance to see them tomorrow."

CHAPTER SEVEN

THE POWER TRUCK pulled up at her house later that evening. Callie was surprised to realize it wasn't even nine yet. After everything that had happened in the past few hours, it felt so much later. After the workers took care of the wire, Matt pulled on his coat. It was still raining lightly. "Do you want to come, too? Or wait here? It's fine either way."

She looked out into the gloom at the tree in her yard, and squeezed her eyes shut. Her earlier bravado had fled. Somehow she wasn't ready to face it. She wasn't strong enough.

"I'll just wait," she murmured, and he leaned in and pressed a quick kiss to her temple. It startled her, but pleased her, too. The gesture was unexpected and sweet. An almost natural extension of the closeness that had developed between them in the past few hours.

He went out in the rain and she watched him carefully pick his way across the street. It wasn't safe for the kids to be outside until that mess was cleaned up. Just as well they'd be at their grandparents' house for the weekend. Matt disappeared around the tree, but she could see the bob of the flashlight.

What seemed like an eternity later, he returned. From the grim set of his face, she knew. She pressed her hand against her mouth, feeling the burn of the hated tears already.

He shucked his jacket and pulled her in for a second time that evening. She didn't fight him, and didn't want to.

"How bad?" she asked, her words muffled against his chest. "Matt, how bad is it?"

She felt him sigh. "The front window is broken, the front porch partially crushed. I can't tell about the roof—the tree is lying on it, but I don't know if it pierced through. I'll need to go up there to check."

The sobs she'd been trying to hold in earlier broke free. He rocked her slightly, and held her tightly. She felt his lips on her hair. "We need to get the window boarded up," he said. "Then I'd like to get a tarp on that roof. Just in case."

She gave a sharp laugh as she stepped back. It had rained so hard for so long. The weatherman had said they'd gotten an inch in just over an hour. "Isn't it too late for that?"

"I don't know," he said softly. "If there are holes, we may be able to contain the water damage."

"Where do I get wood to board it up this time of night?"

"I have some plywood. I bought it for Aldo, the escape artist," Matt admitted. "But I can always get more later. This is far more important."

"I—okay. Okay. I need to think," she muttered, and paced away from him. He fogged her brain, and on top of the stress of the evening, that wasn't a good thing. She was weak right now, vulnerable. And she knew it. "Do you think I can go in now? At the back?"

"Probably. But, Callie—"

"I need to grab a few things," she said. "The bedrooms are at the back of the house. If I could grab their bags and a few things from my room…" Like the pictures of Jason. Her laptop. A few clothes. The panic bubble pressed against her chest. "Please, Matt."

"I'll go in with you," he said firmly.

Rather than waste time arguing, she nodded.

"But first I'm going to put that plywood up," he said. "Then we'll go in."

"All right. Let me help," she said. Now that she knew, she needed to see it. "The boys are asleep. Come here. You need to see this."

She turned and walked down the hall, Matt behind her. She aimed her light in. Aldo lifted his head and wagged his tail slightly, but didn't get up. He'd lain down between the boys, and both kids were curled on their sides facing him.

"Good dog," Matt said softly, and Callie couldn't help but smile when Aldo let out a sigh and closed his eyes again.

"I guess he doesn't want to be disturbed," she whispered, and Matt chuckled quietly.

He waited while she slipped her shoes on and grabbed the too-big jacket. She followed him into the garage and waited while he pulled out hammers and a saw and nails. They hauled that plus the plywood over to her house. Callie gasped at the damage. He hadn't been kidding about the porch. It was splintered and smashed and would need to be entirely replaced. The tree branch that went through the window wasn't huge, but had landed right where she and the kids would have been sitting if they'd been home. Nausea rose up.

Matt touched her arm. "You okay?"

"That branch." She nodded toward the broken window. "It's right where—right where we could have been." The words caught in her throat. Her boys could have been hurt. She tried so hard to protect them—and they could have been hurt right here at home.

He nodded grimly. "I know."

She cleared her throat. "Where do we start? Should I just call Bill?" Jason's brother was a contractor. It all looked like one big mess to her. Overwhelming.

"I can do this part," Matt replied. "But yeah, you'll want to call him soon."

"I'll do it in the morning," she said. If Maureen hadn't done so already. Callie hadn't looked at her phone since she'd called them.

She watched as Matt cut the branch reaching through the window, and pulled it out. Despite her shock and sorrow she couldn't help but notice the flex and play of muscle as he worked. She kept the light trained where he asked her to, and helped nail up the board.

"Done," he said, after the last nail went in. "Let's get the tarp on the roof. Then you can get your things. Do you have a ladder?"

She led the way to the garage. Briefly stymied by nerves and the garage door—of course it wouldn't go up when she hit the button; there was no power—she pointed out the extension ladder and they went back out.

"I'll need your help, if you can manage it," Matt said.

"Ah. Okay." She climbed up the ladder after him and they worked together to get the tarp to cover the worst of it. There were holes up here, too, and that made her heart hurt. She wondered what kind of damage this was doing inside her house.

They put away the ladder in silence, and she went into the kitchen, with him behind her. He flashed his light around and up, and she could see the water damage on the ceiling. Those blasted, useless tears burned again.

She felt Matt squeeze her shoulder in sympathy. "I'll go find the breaker. We'd better turn it off, just in case, to prevent problems when the power comes back on. Is it in the basement?"

"Yes. To your left when you go down the stairs, in the corner."

"All right. Be careful up here," he said as he turned toward the stairs. "There's probably glass all over the living room."

He wasn't wrong. She crunched over the glass and saw the capsized chair and knocked-over TV where the branch had hit. The kids' toy box was overturned, too.

Yes, if they'd been at home, they would have been right here, in this room. It hadn't occurred to her that the tree might come down. The little panic bubble kicked up again. What else hadn't she thought of that was potentially harmful? Could she ever cover all the possibilities?

Shoving her useless thoughts away, she automatically flicked the light switch in the hall, which of course did nothing. She sighed. Just like the kids, who would go in and flick lights when the power went out, confused as to why the switches didn't work.

She hurried toward her room and tripped over a plastic truck that had been abandoned in the middle of the hall. Of course, where else would it be? She gritted her teeth and moved on.

She thanked her lucky stars that she'd been so busy earlier on and had packed both boys' bags. She grabbed them and dropped them in the hall. Then she went back and threw some clothes and toiletries for herself into a bag. She collected her laptop, pictures, and a few photo albums from the living room on her next pass through—just in case the tree came through the roof.

She gathered everything up and picked her way in the dark, since she had no free hands for the flashlight.

Matt was in the kitchen. "Can I take something?"

She relinquished a couple bags without argument and followed him back across the street. It hit her that she was bone-tired. It must have shown on her face, because Matt said, "You can take my room. You'll be more comfortable there."

Callie couldn't imagine sleeping in Matt's bed. It seemed wrong on so many levels she couldn't even fathom them all. "I couldn't run you out of your room."

"You won't be," he assured her. "I can sleep quite comfortably on the couch. Plus I want to get an early crack at that tree tomorrow."

She looked at him, startled. "Oh, Matt. That's not necessary. I can find someone.... My brother-in-law will help. You're not required to take care of us," she said. It seemed like the thing to do, to point that out. For his sake or for hers?

He gave her a small smile. "I know that. I'm not doing it because I have to. I'm doing it because I want to."

"Okay," Callie said, since she was too tired to argue. "Well, I guess I'll go to bed, then." But when she looked up at him, she found herself snared by the intensity of his blue, blue eyes.

She couldn't move even if she'd wanted to, as he edged closer. Her heartbeat picked up so fast she couldn't hear anything over the rush in her ears. He lowered his mouth to hers slowly, pausing just a breath above her lips. Unable to stop herself, she rose up on her toes to meet him for that last little bit and pressed her mouth to his.

He was so solid under her hands, warm and muscular, with the scents of something spicy, and sawdust and rain and fresh air, all mingled together. His lips were gentle, as if maybe he thought she'd bolt if he applied too much pressure.

Need welled up in her, a force that would have knocked her right over if she hadn't been hanging on to him. She made a little noise in her throat and it seemed that was the signal he'd been waiting for. He finally deepened the kiss and she opened to him.

God, it'd been so long since she'd been kissed.

It was that vague thought that acted like a bucket of cold water, and she wrenched herself away with a little gasp. What was she doing? She still wore her husband's rings, for Pete's sake!

"Callie…" His voice was a low rasp, and even as horror filled her, the delicious sound of it made her shiver.

"I—no. I'm going to go to bed," she muttered, and darted around him down the hall, snagging her bag as she went. Cripes. She was going to get in his bed. Without him. But still. That kiss...

She shut the door behind her and rested her head on it, her pulse still hammering and everything in her tingling. What had she done?

The next morning, Matt still wasn't sure what had come over him. He hadn't meant to kiss Callie. Ever. He'd intended to leave her alone, to ignore all this emotional stuff she kept bringing out in him, but apparently he sucked at it. He'd spent all night tossing and turning on the couch over it, and having inappropriate dreams about a buddy's widow, while said widow slept in his bed.

Yeah.

Her brother-in-law, Bill—Jason's big brother—stood with him in front of Callie's house. Callie would be joining them shortly. He hoped like hell the other guy wouldn't pick up on any tension between them.

Bill gave Callie an affectionate hug when she

came over, and Matt had to squash a snap of jealousy. How stupid was that? They were family.

He was not.

Callie didn't really look at him. He caught her gaze once and she turned pink. So she hadn't been unaffected by that kiss, either. Which he'd kind of figured when she'd fled to his room. Without him.

"I called the insurance company last night," she told Bill. "They said they'll be out this morning." Matt glanced at her face again and saw the sadness there. "It looks worse in the daylight," she said, almost to herself.

Bill slipped an arm around her and she leaned on him a little. Matt gritted his teeth. He knew the other man wasn't putting the moves on Callie—he was happily married—but it still got up in Matt's grill to see them touch so familiarly. He shoved his hands in his pockets. Last night she'd leaned on him. Now she wouldn't even look at him. He'd made a hell of a mess of this.

"I'm so sorry, Cal," Bill said. "We'll get it done as fast as possible. I'm going to have the window measured and ordered today." He walked away and Callie's gaze stayed fixed on the roof.

Matt moved in next to her. It was now or never. "I'm sorry about last night," he said quietly. It was true, but not for the reason she'd think. He regretted freaking her out, but not kissing her.

Her head snapped around and there was something that looked a lot like hurt in her eyes. "Don't talk about it. Please. Bill's here." Then she stomped away, back across the street.

Now Matt really felt like a heel. He'd put that look in her eyes. All because he'd just wanted a taste of her. Just one taste.

He was beginning to realize it wasn't going to be enough.

Even though she'd known what to expect, the mess at the house had shocked Callie. Plus she was thrown off balance by Matt and that kiss. The combination had her reeling. Still, the cleanup was well under way. Chain saws were running by seven, and from her neighbor she'd learned the power was expected back on that evening. She called her in-laws to warn them of the mess on the street—mostly small branches—so they'd need to drive carefully. She let the dog out, realizing that he'd need to do his business, then remembered his penchant for escape and went out to stand on the deck while he sniffed around in the backyard. She really missed coffee but there was no way to make any, even if there had been power. She didn't trust herself with Matt's monster of a machine, and she couldn't get her van out to drive even if she'd wanted to go on the hunt for an open coffee shop.

She woke her boys and got breakfast in them. But now she had to show them their house.

"I've got to show you guys something," she told them when they were done with their cereal. "It might be kind of scary, but it will be okay. I promise."

When they went out front, both boys gasped. "Tree fell down," Liam said, his worried eyes a mirror of Eli's.

She hugged them both and pressed kisses to their heads. "Yes, it did," Callie said. "And it broke a window and hurt the porch. There are holes in the roof, too. So we need to do some fixing before we can move back in."

Where would they stay? She pushed that aside for now. One thing at a time.

The kids were concerned, but after Callie assured them the inside was mostly fine, and their toys were fine, they settled down. Though the TV had been hit by the branch and smashed, that didn't seem like a detail they needed to know, since they hadn't specifically asked about it.

"Can we sleep there?" Eli asked. "Or will we sleep at Mr. Matt's?"

The question nearly gave Callie a seizure. Trust a five-year-old to get right to the heart of the matter. "Ah. I'm not sure yet. I'm sure Mr. Matt doesn't want us underfoot."

"But we like Mr. Matt," Eli said.

"And doggie," Liam added.

"I know," she said, steering them back across the street. "But we don't want to be a bother. I'll find somewhere for us to stay. So we'll get the roof and window fixed, and use the back door for a while until we can get the porch replaced."

Assuming there was no structural damage to

the roof, of course. She mentally crossed her fingers it would be fine and stable.

Her in-laws showed up shortly after that. With coffee.

"Oh, bless you," she said, when Maureen offered her the to-go cup.

"It's probably not so hot now," her mother-in-law said ruefully. "But it's caffeine. And Callie—oh my goodness! Look at your poor house!"

Callie sipped the brew. Not superhot, not great, but it tasted wonderful this morning all the same. She swallowed. "I know. It's not as bad as it looks. Really," she added, when Maureen gave her a look. Joe walked around, examining the damage.

"Good thinking on the plywood," he commented. "Where is Matt? Haven't seen that boy in ages."

"Not sure. He can't be too far." To Maureen, she said, "Their things are right here. Luckily, I'd had them already packed. I did throw in an extra couple sets of clothes."

"We don't mind the extra days," Maureen assured her. "We'll be fine. You're coming, too, of course. There's no way you can stay here."

It was tempting to leave, but Callie knew she needed to be close by. Maybe not as close as Matt's house, however. "No, I'm going to stay around here. I need to oversee what's going on. Once the tree's gone and the window's fixed, I'll get the boys back home. Bill's already on it." The benefit of having a contractor in the family.

Maureen frowned. "Where are you going to stay?"

"I'm not sure," Callie admitted. "Probably with Lori." Her boss and friend didn't live close, but it seemed like a better alternative than the temptations that awaited her at Matt's.

Maureen looked as if she was going to argue further, but Matt came around the front of her house. Callie winced and her face heated as their gazes went to him. Would they be able to tell he'd kissed her?

Maureen gasped. "Matt!"

"Mr. and Mrs. M." He moved closer and opened his arms, and Maureen walked right into them.

The embrace was heartfelt and solid, and Callie could see there was real love between them.

"So good to see you," Maureen said, swiping at her eyes. "How have you been?"

They exchanged a few minutes of chitchat, while Callie stood off to the side, trying not to feel guilty, and failing miserably.

Maureen smiled and turned to her husband. "Isn't it wonderful, Joe, that Matt lives here? Right across from Callie and the boys! I have to say, I think Jason would be so pleased." She reached out to Callie and squeezed her arm. "Don't you think so, Callie?"

"Ah." Callie averted her gaze, shame filling her. Would he? After that kiss? She forced herself to meet Maureen's sparkling eyes and say what would clearly make her mother-in-law feel better. "I'm sure he would."

Matt watched Callie send the kids off with her in-laws. The lost look on her face when they drove away made him realize she likely felt abandoned and overwhelmed. Their kiss last night probably hadn't helped, either. He'd make it up to her.

"Stay with me," he said, and she spun around to look at him, clearly incredulous. "I'm serious. There's plenty of room, and you'll be right across the street from your house, so you can keep an eye on it." He wanted to add he wouldn't touch her, but he wasn't so sure about that. He wouldn't blame her if she didn't trust him. Hell, he didn't trust himself anymore.

She chewed on her lip for a minute, clearly torn, which was a small blow to his ego. "I—all right. I will. But just until I can find somewhere else."

"Fair enough," he said, and moved around her to grab his water bottle. His arm brushed hers— barely—and he felt her tense. It would definitely be best to have her find somewhere else to stay as soon as possible. Otherwise they'd both be on pins and needles around each other.

"What do you want to do with all this wood?" he asked. "You've got enough for your fireplace, plus plenty more."

She looked at the tree and shook her head. "I have no use for it."

"Your fireplace is gas?"

"No. It's wood. But I don't light fires," she answered, not looking at him. "Not anymore."

Matt cursed himself for being so dense. Jason had died in a blaze, trying to save a fellow firefighter. Stood to reason Callie would steer clear of fire of any sort. "All right. I can arrange for this to be taken away, if you want."

She nodded, still not meeting his eyes. "That's fine. Thanks."

Callie didn't have to be at the salon until nine-thirty, so she insisted on helping with the tree. She'd found gloves in the garage and wouldn't let him talk her out of it. She hauled what she could out of the way as he cut it. The process was tedious and loud, so they didn't talk much over the whine of the chain saw, but that was okay, too. They fell into a kind of comfortable rhythm. When they stopped to take a water break, he looked at her. Really looked at her. She was flushed, disheveled, and a few strands of hair had escaped her ponytail. He thought he'd never seen anything sexier than Callie standing there, her shirt damp with sweat and streaked with grime, her hair a little messy and her total focus on the job they were doing.

While he would never wish this kind of thing on anyone, he wasn't sorry he was able to go through it with her. But he needed to keep his focus on the chain saw, so he kept his gaze off her as much as possible. Plus he didn't want to spook her, since she'd be staying at his place for a couple days.

With no kids.

He was a gentleman. Or rather, he would be, even if it killed him.

CHAPTER EIGHT

TWO DAYS OF staying at Matt's, and Callie was pretty sure she was going to lose her mind.

Not just from the stress of the situation at her house, but from being away from her kids and being in such close contact with Matt.

She welcomed the hours at her job so she could breathe. Bill had gotten right to work on her place, so the repairs were going quickly. Roof and window were the priorities, and the water damage inside had been minimal, but there was stuff that had to be replaced in the attic. She was looking at a week or so out of her home, if all went according to plan.

She lay on her air mattress now, in the bedroom where the boys had slept. It was better than the couch, far better than Matt's way-too-comfy bed, which smelled yummy like him. This room had a door, and if she wanted it, a lock. Not that Matt had given her any reason to think she'd need it.

No, it was her she didn't trust.

Since he'd kissed her, everything had changed. They'd managed to avoid talking about it, and Callie tried very hard to pretend it hadn't happened, but utterly failed.

So she kind of tiptoed around him and he gave her the space she needed.

It was both kind and infuriating.

Aldo padded into her room and looked at her. He liked her air mattress for his own personal use and seemed a bit nonplussed to find her on it.

She chuckled as she held out a hand, which he sniffed carefully. "Sorry, boy. It's mine for now." She rolled to a seated position and then stood up to lead him out of the room, closing the door behind her and earning a *really?* look from the dog.

Matt would be home in half an hour. This seemed like a good time to go to the store for something. Anything. But when she went outside, he was just pulling into the driveway.

Oh, no.

The nerves kicked up, her belly a crazy riot of

them as she watched him unfold himself from the truck. She realized she was clutching her purse in front of her like a safety device, and made herself relax her grip.

"Hi," he said, and she realized she'd been staring at him. She swallowed and managed a smile.

"Hi. I was just, um…" She waved vaguely at her van and Matt raised a brow.

"Running away?"

She took a step back, let out what even to her ears sounded like a nervous laugh. She hadn't expected him to be so direct. "I—of course not. From what?"

He looked right at her. *Through* her. "Me."

Her heart fluttered. Well, she'd asked, hadn't she? "It's been a little awkward," she admitted, since avoiding the subject when he was being straightforward seemed silly.

"Yeah," he agreed, turning toward the house, then back to her. "Callie. I'm sorry I kissed you. I get that you aren't ready. It won't happen again."

While she knew she should be relieved, a low swell of disappointment ran through her. Of course he was right. It wouldn't—couldn't—happen again. She didn't want it to any more than he did. And it was just as awkward for him to be here with her as vice versa. So really, she needed to chalk up her mixed feelings to all the stress she was under right now and leave it at that.

"It's okay," she said to his retreating back. Then she looked at the car keys in her hand, sighed and got into her van. The least she could do was grab some actual groceries, since takeout was wearing thin—and getting expensive.

After she pulled into a parking space at the grocery store she called her mother-in-law and waited for her to pick up.

"Hi," said Eli, and Callie smiled, even as her heart squeezed. She missed her little guys so much.

"Hi, honey! How are you?"

There was a pause. Breathing. Prompting by Maureen in the background. "Um. Fine." Callie couldn't help but grin. They could talk a mile a minute, but on the phone—unless it was about Lego sets or dogs—nada.

"That's good, honey."

"Is Aldo there?"

Ah. Kid priorities. "No. He's back home." She winced. "I mean, back at Matt's house. I'm in the van right now."

"'Kay." Scrambling noises, then Maureen's laughing voice. "He went to tell Liam the dog wasn't there. Just like their daddy, always wanting a dog." There was both sorrow and humor in her tone.

"I know," Callie said with a sigh. Between the dog, her kids and the man, she was being hit from all sides by things she wasn't ready for.

"So how is it? Bill said it'll be another week or so, right? How are you holding up?"

Callie didn't think it was acceptable to tell her mother-in-law she was a nervous wreck thanks to her sexy neighbor and the tense undercurrents between them. "Oh, fine."

Something in her voice must have given her away, because Maureen made a little noise. "Matt not being a good host?"

Her eyes widened, even though Maureen couldn't see her. "Oh, no, he's just fine. It was very nice of him to let me stay. I don't see him much. We're both pretty busy." Then she wondered what had made her add that last part. Had it sounded as if she was trying to assure Maureen there was nothing going on?

"Matt's a wonderful man. We haven't seen him much, but he was all over the world for so many years. So very glad he's home now, and close to you. I have to say, it makes me feel better to know that."

Callie stared at the dashboard. That comment seemed like a minefield. Maybe it meant nothing, maybe it meant too much. Maybe she was overthinking it due to a guilty conscience. Most likely the latter. "Ah. Well, that's good."

The rest of the conversation was less awkward, much to her relief. Before hanging up, Callie talked to both boys one more time and promised to call again at bedtime.

She tucked the phone back into her purse and sat for a minute, frowning at the steering wheel. Maureen had almost sounded as if she'd encourage her to start a relationship with Matt. That couldn't be right. Deciding she'd misunderstood, and was affected by the kiss they'd shared, Callie got out of her van. Matt wasn't her type. Another risk-taking man wasn't a possibility. She'd had enough of that to last her a lifetime.

Still. A part of her knew she was being a little bit hypocritical. She'd been pretty adventurous once upon a time herself. But after Jason's death, she'd lost that part of her. Well, no, to be more accurate, she'd given it up. It was no way to live when she had children relying on her—and she couldn't risk her boys losing her, too.

Matt watched Callie leave, then went into the house. She was right not to trust him, but it still sucked to have her run away like that. Was it better that she admitted it? He wasn't sure.

He went for a run with Aldo, and when he came back, her van was in his driveway. In the house, he smelled beef cooking and heard the TV going in the kitchen. His stomach growled. Aldo plodded down the hall and dropped in front of her closed door. Matt toed off his running shoes and laughed at the dog.

"She foil you, big boy?"

Aldo turned big eyes to him, then to the door, obviously expecting Matt to open it so he could

have access to the blow-up mattress. Matt shook
his head and Aldo shut his eyes, clearly disappointed with his human.

Still chuckling, Matt went into his kitchen. It
struck him this was the first time the house had
smelled like real food since he'd moved in. That
was pathetic. He really needed to learn to cook.
Something that smelled this good.

"Smells great in here," he said, and Callie spun
around, eyes wide. She slapped a hand over her
heart.

"Oh! I didn't hear you come in." She scrambled
for the TV remote, but he grabbed her hand. She
went perfectly still at the contact.

"It's fine," he said, and let her go. She snatched
her hand back as if she'd burned it on her pan,
and he tried not to take it personally. "What are
you making?"

Clearly on safer ground, she went back to the
stove. "Just a stir-fry. Beef and broccoli. Easy
but really good. My kids love it." She sent him
a glance that was almost playful. A nice change
from the wary look from earlier. "So will you."

"Okay." He sat at the counter and let himself

enjoy the view of her in his kitchen, the smells and sounds that made a home a *home*. Things he'd been missing for twenty years. That he remembered from growing up.

He'd loved being in the army, loved the unpredictability, but yet the strict routine of it all. Until those last two tours in Afghanistan. He'd seen too much, done too much, to go back. It'd finally worn him down.

She moved to the broccoli and pulled out a cutting board. He stared at it for a minute, frowning. "I have one of those?"

She laughed. A real laugh, full and bawdy and rolling. If he'd been standing, the sound would have sent him to his knees. God, if she'd laugh like that more often, he'd say asinine things every damn day.

Still chuckling, and apparently not noticing what she'd done to him, she plopped the head of broccoli on the cutting board, little droplets of water flying around her. "No, you do not. It's mine. As are the knives, the spices and the pans." She turned and cocked a brow at him. "Since your selection of cooking stuff is a little, shall we say, sparse."

"Guilty," he agreed. "Kitchen implements weren't something I carried around with me." What would he have done with a frying pan in the army?

She began chopping broccoli, her movements neat and efficient. "No, I'm sure they weren't," she agreed. "But maybe you want to invest in a couple now just in case you get sick of takeout."

She had him there. He watched as she scooped up the sliced florets and dumped them in the pan, her back again to him as she stirred it together. Her apron tails draped over her ass in a way that made his mouth water.

Whoa. He quickly jerked his eyes back up to the middle of her back. Time to refocus.

"What's in the other pan?" he asked, trying to distract himself.

"Noodles," she answered. "My kids prefer them to rice. Made them out of habit, I guess." She clapped the lid on the stir-fry. "This'll be about five minutes."

So he'd eat, then shower. By then he'd need a cold one.

She bustled around, draining noodles, getting plates. The plates weren't paper, so she'd obviously brought them with her, as well. She dished the food up and they ate at the counter. Wow, had he ever missed real cooking. He got home-cooked meals so rarely, they were a real treat. And this woman had given him two in less than a week.

Best not to get used to it, because, like her, they weren't for him. Casting for a safe topic, he said, "Aldo bugging you?"

She looked up, confusion in her caramel eyes. "Now?"

"Anytime. He's camped in front of your door." Matt inclined his head, and she got up with a frown and walked over so she could see the dog. She was chuckling when she came back.

"No, he's not a bother. He just thinks my bed is his. And he seems sort of confused as to why I don't share."

"Sorry about that," Matt said. They were making headway on training, but sometimes Aldo knew what he wanted and was pretty stubborn. Especially, apparently, when it came to Callie and her kids. Though frankly, Matt didn't blame Aldo for wanting to share her bed—so did he, for entirely different reasons. He'd be happy if she opted to leave the mattress for the dog, and share his room. *Focus.* "He's got manners, but they seem to be a little sporadic."

"It's fine." Callie took a bite and he watched her chew, then swallow. The actions weren't in and of themselves sexy, but somehow she made them seem that way.

He was in a boatload of trouble, if he didn't get this under control, and quick.

"Leave the dishes, please," he said, because he knew she'd clean up if he didn't expressly ask her not to. "You cooked, I'll clean. It's only fair."

She stared at him, then shook her head. "I'm imposing on you. This is the least I can do. And I don't mind the cleaning."

He rubbed a hand over his head. Frustrating woman. "Then at least wait for me. I'm going to shower first, and I'll help. The water heater can't do both." It was a low blow, insinuating there wasn't enough water—it was probably true, though—but he wanted to be around her more.

She relented, but likely because she recognized the rudeness of taking hot water from his shower. "Okay."

He bathed quickly, trying to keep his thoughts off her and not using nearly as much hot water as normal, since his thoughts were still running pretty hot from his unintended houseguest and her fantastic laugh.

Among other things.

Callie waited for Matt to finish, scraping the plates and pans, decanting leftovers into containers she'd brought over for the fridge and trying to determine if the dishwasher worked. Even if it did, there appeared to be no dishwasher soap. Really, if he ate takeout on paper plates—and how sad was that?—a couple forks and a glass each day weren't enough to run the dishwasher, unless he wanted to wait a whole week or two to run it.

Plus, being busy took her mind off him in the shower. All those muscles, under the hot water.

Oh, my.

Callie tried to bring her thoughts back around to mundane matters, but it wasn't easy. This was a terrible time for her hormones to have made a reappearance. They'd been shut down, as they should be, after her husband's death.

She touched her rings. When would it be time to take them off? How would she know? Was the fact she had these feelings for Matt enough? The problem was, she wasn't certain they were real and here to stay. How would she know for sure?

The bathroom door opened and Callie trained her attention on the entertainment program on the TV. She heard him, then caught a whiff of his soap and shampoo, a yummy combo that was spicy and fresh. That low tug was back, that wanting what she couldn't have.

She was glad she had her back to him so he couldn't see her shut her eyes for a moment. When she turned around, she hoped he couldn't read her expression very well.

"How was your shower?"

He came closer and her mouth watered—actually watered. "Fine. Ready?"

"I, um, wasn't sure if the dishwasher works,"

she said, trying to hold on to her sanity a little longer.

"I'm told it does," he said. "But I've never needed it."

"I can tell," she muttered, then blushed when he laughed. "I'm sorry. That was rude."

"Not at all." He turned the water on and gave a squirt of soap. "You want to dry?"

They worked in a fairly companionable silence. Callie was very careful not to touch him, until they both reached for a pan and his fingers slid over hers. She swallowed a little gasp and her eyes flew to his.

He was looking at her in that way. With desire, hunger, confusion. Longing. No doubt what was present in her own eyes, too, because she felt it all in her heart.

Awareness arced between them, hot and bright, almost a visible thing. She could barely breathe as they stood there for one heartbeat, then two, then three. Then she blinked and pulled her fingers out from under his, shaking as she turned away.

"Callie." His voice was rough and sent a delicious shiver up her spine. She squeezed her eyes shut tightly, trying to get herself back under control. How did he affect her so quickly? With a slight touch, a look? He moved closer, but didn't touch her. Her breath picked up and she couldn't make herself move. Wasn't sure her knees would hold her if she tried to step away.

She heard the rasp of his breathing, felt the warmth as it stirred her hair. She turned her head to him just as he leaned in and pressed a kiss to her temple.

Then her upper jaw.

Then another, a little lower.

He didn't touch her with his hands. She knew she could leave, if her feet would just let her. If she could release her death grip on the counter. Her heart pounded so hard she was afraid it would carry her away.

Instead, she turned her head and met his mouth with her own. His kiss was light, feathery, a question. Asking for permission without saying a word. She paused for just a moment, letting him play, then giving in because she couldn't help it. Because she wanted it, too.

She opened to him, let him deepen the kiss, felt the reverberation of his low groan as he stroked her tongue with his. He still hadn't touched her, and somehow, that made it hotter.

Then his hand came up and slid over her cheek, cupping her face. The touch was featherlight, soft, reverent, a direct contrast to the urgency of his mouth.

Callie gave in. All of her. She pressed against him, slid her arms around him and felt the pounding of his heart under her breasts. Heard his sharp intake of breath as he pulled away to angle his head to go deeper. She whimpered, not from fear but because, God, she'd missed this. This connection with another person. Intimacy, on all its levels.

"God, Callie," he whispered against her mouth, before diving back in, and she held on to him because she fully understood what he meant, what he hadn't said, what she couldn't say.

When she finally drew away, he laid her head on his chest with his hand and she squeezed her eyes shut, listening to the thump of his heart, the unsteadiness of his breathing, both of which matched her own. She felt the press of his arousal against her, and her answering need. But she wasn't ready to go there. Not yet. A week ago, even this much passion hadn't been on her radar. Now—well, now she needed to figure out what was going on.

"Wow," he said finally. "Callie. I know I said I wouldn't, but—"

"I know." She pulled away, now fairly certain of her ability to walk. "It's okay, Matt. I—wanted it, too. I'm going to let you finish these, since we're almost there, anyway. I'll put them away later."

She dropped her towel on the counter and walked away, feeling his eyes on her, but knew he wouldn't follow her. This situation didn't make him any happier than it did her. She knew that.

She stepped over the dog and shut the door to the bedroom. Flicked on the light and sank on her mattress, staring at the blank walls, the bare windows. Even with her bedside lamp—the overhead was too harsh—the room wasn't cozy.

She rubbed her hands over her face. This was getting out of control. Her body still hummed from his kisses, from her reaction to them. From how badly she wanted. Wanted what? She didn't want to want him. It wasn't part of her life right now, wasn't on her list of things to do. She'd been fully prepared to go this alone. But Matt had turned everything upside down. Or rather, her feelings for Matt had. It wasn't his fault. He wasn't forcing her to feel this way.

She just didn't know what to do about it, how to get it all back under control. If, at this point, it was even possible. Every time he kissed her, they moved a little closer to the point of no return. She was fooling herself if she thought she could hold her heart in reserve. She knew she'd never just "mess around" with anyone—too much was at stake for her and her kids.

CHAPTER NINE

THE REST OF the tree had been long cleared, so the trucks parked in front of Callie's house, with their ladders and toolboxes, were a welcome sight. It meant work was getting done. The boys were coming back tomorrow, and while they'd all have to pack into that rear bedroom at Matt's house, Callie was okay with that. Matt had offered to clear his fitness equipment out of the third bedroom, but she had declined. They wouldn't be here that much longer, and she wasn't going to impose on him any more than she already had.

Plus the kids were a wonderful, living, breathing barrier between her and Matt. She needed that. Unfortunately. Since she wasn't doing so great on her own. As the smoking-hot kiss yesterday had proved. A little shiver ran through her at the memory.

Matt was odd. He didn't want her to be close,

yet he'd drawn her right in. As if they were two magnets, unable to stay apart. It was unnerving. She didn't know what had happened to him in Afghanistan, although it was obviously something traumatic. He wasn't willing to talk about it. And she wouldn't push.

She went to work, pleased that it was warm enough for her to leave her heavy coat at home. *At Matt's. Not home.* As March moved to April, it was wonderful to need only a light jacket rather than the down parka she usually wore.

"A full one today," Lori observed when Callie came into the salon. "Funny how it goes like that, isn't it? Not that I'm complaining."

Callie laughed. "Me, either."

The day's paper was folded on the counter and Callie picked it up to put it in the reception area. The front page article caught her eye: Afghan Army Vets Open Local Adventure Company.

Right under the headline was a photo of Matt, with his sexy smile and crinkles around his eyes. The other man was handsome, too, but Callie barely looked at him. Under that was a picture of Matt in his fatigues, crouched down, talking to a child. Her heart squeezed.

"Hmm. Hot," Lori commented from behind her. "No wonder you were drooling. I'm thinking I could use more adventure in my life."

Callie felt the blush crawl up her neck. "Lori."

"Actually, check that. You could use more adventure in *your* life. Are they single? If so, why don't you sign up for one?"

This time Callie gasped. "What? No way."

"No way on the man or the adventure?"

"Both." She hesitated, then pointed at Matt's photo. "That's the guy whose house I'm staying at."

Lori's eyes widened, then turned speculative. "Well, well, well. Callie Marshall. I guess I've been asking the wrong questions, haven't I?"

"It's nothing," she assured her friend. Well, nothing other than a few kisses and this constant inner turmoil. "Just convenient, because he lives right across the street from me."

Lori stared at her, and Callie could see all the pieces clicking into place. "This is him," she said slowly. "The new neighbor with the dog. Jason's friend.

"Jason's old friend," she admitted, feeling a wave of shame. Lori didn't know the half of it.

Lori squealed and threw her arms around her. "That's wonderful!"

"What? How?" Callie pulled back and stared at her, sure she'd lost her mind. There was nothing wonderful about this, even if Matt did make her feel—well, wonderful. Except for this awful guilt.

"There are no coincidences," Lori said simply. "You need each other. I'm sure of it."

Callie dropped the paper on the table. Sad to say, she didn't agree. "That's a lovely thought, but I don't think so. If nothing else, look. His life is all about risk-taking—it's like he couldn't get enough of it in the army. I can't deal with that again after how I lost Jason. You of all people should know that."

"I know you believe that. And I think you're wrong." When Callie drew back, shocked, Lori touched her hand. "Hear me out. Life is full of risk. Love is a risk. You can't protect yourself—

or your boys—from all life's dangers forever. Maybe Matt's not the right man for you, that's fine. But you aren't doing yourself or your kids any favors by staying away from him—or any other man—just because of his job or what he enjoys doing in his spare time, even. Think about it."

Callie stared at her as she walked away. Lori was wrong. She could protect them, all of them, from further sorrow and loss. If she just held them tight enough, close enough, she could keep it all at bay.

Couldn't she?

In the salon, two women were chatting. Callie was pretty preoccupied, but when they mentioned Out There Adventures, Matt's company, her attention snapped back to them. One of the women had the paper in her lap while she waited for her color to set.

"So my son works there," Callie's client, Mrs. Hensen, said, inclining her head toward the paper. "He's going to be a guide this summer. He can't wait. He loves the outdoors and the kind of activities this company specializes in. It's a perfect fit. Matt and Brice have done such a great job getting it ready to go."

Callie wanted to ask her how she could let her child embark on such a dangerous job. Even if he was an adult, shouldn't she be able to talk him out of it? Steer him to something safer? What would she do if something happened to him? Did he have a family that needed him? Not that Callie doubted Matt was making things as safe as possible. But something like that, extreme sports, had risks embedded in them. It was part of the draw, what made it so exciting. And a huge part of what scared her silly and made Matt so off-limits.

"I've heard that," the second woman remarked. "Too bad I'm not thirty years younger." Both women giggled like schoolgirls.

Callie dropped the scissors into the cleaning solution with a clatter. Both ladies looked at her and she smiled in apology. This was probably not the time to say she was living with Matt. Even temporarily.

They resumed their conversation and Callie wiped off her station. Time to finish Mrs. Hensen, who was still talking to her friend. "I've told my daughter maybe she should sign up for a tour. Brice is married, but Matt's not. Looks to me like Matt Bowden might be just the thing to take her mind off her stupid cheating ex."

Both women laughed again. Callie kept her face neutral and her hands steady as she removed Mrs. Hensen's rollers. Matt wasn't a toy, something to be used and tossed aside. Or an object to be lusted after. Though, well, to be perfectly honest, Callie wasn't doing so well on that last point herself!

She stifled a sigh. Her outrage was misplaced, and qualified as overreacting. Matt was an adult. And frankly, if it brought business in, he might very well welcome women on the prowl. She didn't know him well enough to say.

And she certainly did not care.

Though she seemed to need the reminder. Especially when the memory of his mouth on hers surfaced all too frequently and made her feel dizzy.

She got Mrs. Hensen all fixed up and out the

door with a smile on her face. Good. She'd be a return customer. Whether Callie opted to open her own place or not, it was good to build her client list, both for her sake and Lori's. The conversation she'd overheard bugged her a little bit, though, even after the women had left.

"Hmm," Lori commented as she swept up the last of the hair from her own client. "Why didn't you tell them he lives by you? Or that you know him?"

Callie laughed. "I don't want to be responsible for the parade of women to his door. And the extra traffic on our street…" She shook her head in mock outrage.

Lori leaned on her broom, her eyes sparkling. "Or maybe you don't want the competition?"

Callie gaped at her friend. "Lori! How can you—what a thing to say."

Lori patted her shoulder. "I was kidding, my dear. But your reaction is very interesting." She cocked her head to the side, and now there was a teasing, knowing glint in her eyes. "Don't you think?"

"Not really," Callie murmured. Darn it. Lori

was right. She'd been a bit too vehement. Not because she thought there'd be competition—that implied there was something there to compete for, and there wasn't. But where had that sour feeling in her stomach come from? The thought of Mrs. Hensen's daughter trying to hook up with Matt? Crazy.

Callie would have to watch herself very carefully now. She turned to drop her wet towels in the bin. And what was up with people pushing her toward Matt? All of a sudden, it seemed everyone had picked up on the chemistry between them, without even seeing them together! Maybe she was giving off some kind of fix-me-up vibe and didn't know it?

She'd tried so hard to stay neutral on the subject of Matt. But it was exhausting. Her feelings toward him weren't neutral. There was no denying that. She wasn't sure what they were, exactly, and maybe didn't even want to know. There was a definite physical connection, but it was more than just that. More than a shared connection to the past.

But she did know it scared her.

* * *

When she got home that evening, she had a new front window. She pulled into Matt's driveway and ran across the street to see it, happiness and relief filling her.

"Yay," she murmured. Measurable progress. This was a big step toward moving back in. Toward getting back to normal. Though, as she heard Matt's car pull in behind her, she had to admit *normal* had been turned on its ear lately.

"Look at that. Bill works fast," Matt observed as he came up behind her.

"Yes, he does. Thank God." Then as it hit her how her words might sound, she half turned to Matt. "I'm sorry, I didn't mean it quite like that."

He slanted her an amused look. "I know."

"I'm very grateful to you for everything, but I'm looking forward to being back home." *Which doesn't smell like you. Where I don't run into you early in the morning. Where I'm safe from all these unwanted feelings.*

"I know that, too," he agreed, and to her relief, he didn't pursue it any further. "Did Bill say when they could start on the roof?"

Here was the rub. "Next week." It was four days before he could get to it. Callie hadn't pushed, because she knew he was busy, and they all thought she was in such a good place at Matt's house. Which, technically, she was. And she couldn't really say anything to make them think differently.

If they only knew about those fantastic kisses, however, things would change.

"So we'll be around a few more days, I'm afraid," she said, not looking at Matt, afraid he'd read her thoughts on her face.

"I have no problem with that," he assured her. "Neither does Aldo."

To be fair, he'd gotten used to having her around. He'd been on his own for so long, having another person—actually, multiple people, including kids—in his space had been unnerving at first, but now he liked it.

Callie kept to herself, taking all her shower stuff back with her into her room—trying to make herself as small as possible, he thought. But there'd been one day when he'd gotten in there and seen her shampoo next to his. It'd been a silly thing, but it had somehow pleased him.

He'd even opened the bottle and taken a sniff, and the now-familiar scent of vanilla had hit him hard. It made him think of kissing her the other day, how if he was close enough he could get a whiff of her hair right now.

It was almost enough to push him toward madness.

But that had been the only time she'd done that. Just as well.

Now, she gave him a little smile, her shields firmly in place. *Stay away*, her body language practically screamed. He honored that by keeping a little bit of distance between them. "That's good. Maybe you'll have to buy Aldo an air mattress of his own after all this."

He laughed as they turned to walk back over to his house. The mutt would love that. "Yeah, maybe."

The smell of food caught him off guard when he unlocked the door and stepped aside for her to go first. "Smells great. Were you cooking?"

She shook her head. "Sort of. I started something in the slow cooker this morning. It's nice to come home to dinner already done." She shot him a look as she toed off her shoes. "Maybe you need one. Drop something in, turn it on, done for when you get home from work."

"Maybe," he said, thinking it was probably still too much for just one guy. And then, as he watched her pad across the floor, stopping to rub a very happy Aldo on the head, then continuing to the kitchen to lift the top and check what was in the pot, a little truth bubbled up. Matt really liked having her here. It wasn't just that he'd adjusted to it, tolerated it. He liked how she looked in his space—not out of place, but as if she belonged. Not to mention he missed those boys of hers when they weren't around.

Aldo nudged Matt's hand and whimpered, reminding him that he needed to go out. Callie turned around and caught him staring at her. The heat stirred between them, the physical pull almost a visible thing. He didn't move toward her, though it took far more effort than it should have not to. She looked away, and even from here he could see the agitated rise and fall of her chest. She cleared her throat.

"Looks like he's ready for a break," she observed, with a smile for the dog, and something in Matt slipped, shifted. Something he hadn't known was there. It was gone just as fast, but he still felt odd. As if something completely out of his control had just changed.

"Yeah. Let's go outside, boy," he said gruffly, grateful for a few minutes to figure out what had just happened.

What made him a little nervous was that Callie herself didn't seem out of place in his house or in his kitchen. In his life. Except, she had belonged to Jason. Having feelings for his friend's widow seemed wrong. How could Matt consider taking over his family? Stepping in and filling his friend's shoes gave him a strong feeling of guilt. Not to mention he didn't really know anything about kids, much less how to be a father.

How could he even contemplate this? His fiancée had broken it off with him, after accusing him of being unable to fully commit to her. He hadn't meant to hold himself in reserve, but apparently he'd gotten so used to being on his own that he'd been unable to really let another person into his heart and mind. So how could he possibly make it work with a ready-made family?

He let the dog out and went with him into the backyard, needing a few minutes of space to mull everything over. Another thing. The very nature of his business meant he'd be gone a lot, often in places where there was no cell phone reception. Callie needed someone who could be around for her, for the kids, all the time. A true partner. She deserved nothing less. Matt wasn't sure how to be that, if he could. Or even if he wanted to be.

He shoved it all out of his mind and whistled for Aldo. He wasn't getting anywhere close to resolving this problem simply by turning it over and over in his mind. He'd let it go for now.

"Matt, you've got a visitor," Marley said, popping into his office. Her eyes were shining and she looked smug as she leaned forward and whispered, "It's Callie! Matt, she's so cute!"

Matt inwardly cringed. He'd mentioned to Brice he'd invited Callie and her kids to stay, and regretted it right away, because of course Brice had to go and tell Marley, who was over the moon with joy for all the wrong reasons.

"Don't let her hear you say that," he warned, and Marley gave him a little smile with big eyes. He sighed. He wasn't fooled by her innocence. This woman was a force to be reckoned with.

He followed her out into the main office area. It wasn't the kind that people often came to, since so much of their business took place out of town, even out of state. Because of this, there weren't comfy chairs or anything that went in a regular reception area.

"Callie," he said, spotting her examining a beautiful action photo of white-water rafters on the Menominee River with clear concern. "What brings you here?"

She spun around and the worried look on her face faded away. There was a fleeting glimpse of pleasure when she spotted him, but it left so fast he wasn't sure he'd seen it. "Matt. Sorry to bother you," she added. "I left the house key on the kitchen counter this morning. I need to get in and pick up something I forgot."

Marley stepped around Matt, apparently giving up on his manners. "Hi, Callie. I'm Marley, Brice's wife and Matt's old friend." Unperturbed by his sigh, she flashed her a brilliant smile.

"Hi, Marley." Callie extended her hand and they shook.

"Don't worry, he's all bark, no bite," Marley said, in that charming way she had of interfering, but making it impossible to be angry with her. "I'll let you two chat." And she was gone almost as fast as she'd come in.

"I like her," Callie said to him, and he nodded.

"Most people do."

Her brow quirked and humor flashed in her eyes. "Just most?"

He huffed out a sigh. "She's a great person, just a little interfering. She means well." Marley didn't see that just because she and Brice were happily married, it wasn't necessarily the right path for everyone. It sure wasn't for him. "So. You want to head back and I'll let you in?"

Callie turned a little pink. "I'm really sorry. I don't want to bother you."

"No bother. Hang on." He went in the back to let Brice know he'd be gone for a bit, and ignored

Marley's innocent remark about there being no reason to hurry. Back in the main area, he found Callie examining another photo, this one of a mountain biker.

"Great pics, aren't they?" he asked as he came up behind her. "That one is Brice, actually. The white-water one is from a trip in the Upper Peninsula we took last time I was home. It was that trip that set us on this path, actually. What do you think?"

"I think it looks extremely dangerous," Callie said quietly, and his stomach dropped. Of course she would think so. He already knew she was risk averse. Seeing hard evidence of what he did wasn't going to win points with her, even though she'd enjoyed stuff like that once, herself.

"It is," he agreed, thinking it was probably best to confront her concerns head-on rather than dance around them. "You've been white-water rafting. You know what it's like. But we minimize as much of the danger as possible. It's always risky, but we're never reckless." There was a huge difference, to his mind. Risks were calculated and planned for and mitigated. "Reckless" was charging ahead with no thought to the consequences. And they never, ever did that.

"I can't afford to take any chances anymore," she said as she walked ahead of him out the door. "And as far as I can tell, there's no difference between risky and reckless. Both are going forward and saying to hell with the consequences."

He wasn't going to argue with her, but her words and slightly bitter tone bothered him. "I'm sorry you feel that way," was all he said. He could not be involved with a woman who wouldn't accept this very core part of who he was. He loved the rush and yes, the edge of danger, but would never put himself or another person into danger knowingly. He wasn't stupid. But realizing she had major issues about how Jason had died, while working in a dangerous job he loved, Matt didn't know if he could help her move past it.

She gave a little shrug and got in her van, waiting to follow him back to the house. He wondered if he could show her what they did, on a small scale. Maybe it would help her to see that some slight measure of risk was okay. She didn't have to go all-in, but perhaps she could begin to see

that there was nothing wrong with taking calculated risks, especially if you thought everything
through beforehand. But maybe it wasn't his call.
On the other hand, what would Jason want her
to do? Want Matt to do? He wouldn't want her
to hide away from life forever, that was for sure.
Maybe he owed it to his friend to help her not
be so afraid.

Otherwise, how could she ever move forward?

CHAPTER TEN

"I'M SORRY, CALLIE, it's going to be a few more days." Bill's tone the next day was apologetic, but rushed. "There's some water damage to the attic. It won't take long, but it will add some time, on top of the roof delay."

Her heart sank right down to her toes. Oh, no. "It's okay, Bill, don't worry about it," she said, keeping her voice cheerful. What was a few more days of living in Matt's house?

Besides torture?

She was a big girl. She could handle it.

Bill explained that some of the supplies needed had been delayed, but he hoped to have them late next week. Callie hung up, grateful she'd taken the call in her van as she was going on her lunch hour. She needed to figure out what they were going to do now. It didn't seem right to ask Matt if they could stay another week or so.

Frustration coursed through her. She wasn't upset with Bill; he'd rushed her job to the fore-front of his busy schedule, and she was grateful. Delays like this weren't in his control. No, it was the whole situation that had her on edge.

The kids were due home this evening, so she hurried back to Matt's. There wasn't much she could do for them, other than roll out their sleep-ing bags and arrange a few of their favorite toys to make it seem cozier. Maybe it was enough to help it feel like an adventure for them. Who was she kidding? They'd be fine. Frankly, the novelty of living with Aldo was enough to keep them happy.

Her cell rang again as she was pulling into the grocery store for a couple boxes of the boys' fa-vorite cereals. It was Maureen.

"Hi, Callie. Bill told us the news about the sup-plies," she said. "Do you want to come here until it's all done? Instead of us bringing the boys back tonight?"

"Ah." Callie's first instinct was to say yes. Get away from Matt, from the feelings. But it really wasn't practical to stay with her in-laws;

she needed to be closer to home and work. "No. Thanks, though. We'll be okay for now. I like being able to see what's going on over there. Plus it's closer to the salon."

"That's fine, of course," Maureen said. "Whatever works best for you. Just keep us in mind, in case things change. Is everything okay at Matt's?"

Hmm. This was a trick question, so Callie chose her words carefully. "Oh, absolutely fine. He's been very generous. It's just a lot to ask of him, to take us all in for so long." Not to mention all the weird tensions and vibes, and pretending they weren't attracted to each other, had them both on edge. But that was no topic for a discussion with her mother-in-law. "So I'll talk to him tonight."

"I understand. He's a good man, Callie. Okay, well, the kids are eager to see you. So we'll meet you later."

They confirmed the details and hung up. Callie ran her errands and got back to the salon in time for her next appointment. A walk-in, as it turned out. Marley.

The woman lit up when she saw her, even as Callie's heart sank just a little bit. Marley had made no secret of the fact that she viewed Callie as a potential girlfriend for Matt. Finding her here today was almost too much.

Still, she returned the other woman's smile. It was impossible not to. There was no hint of prurient curiosity in her eyes. Callie suspected that with Marley, what you saw was what you got, and she seemed generous and kind.

"So what do you need done today?" Callie asked, hoping that maybe they could keep the conversation off Matt.

"A trim. My old stylist moved to California, and I'm in the market for a new one. I've heard good things about Time For You, so I thought I'd try here first." Marley's smile was open, and Callie felt bad about suspecting the other woman had ulterior motives in being here. "I didn't know you worked here, if that's what you were thinking."

"Ah. I wondered," she admitted as she hooked the cape around her new client's shoulders. Because if Marley was going to be honest with her, she deserved it in return.

"Nope. It's a nice surprise. So." Marley lifted her short blond locks with her fingers. "It's about an inch too long. I've been busy and haven't gotten to it. Plus, like I said, I was abandoned by my longtime stylist." Her quick grin showed she had no hard feelings.

"All right. Let's see what we can do." Callie listened as she explained what she liked and why, then led her to the sinks for a shampoo.

They chatted as she washed Marley's hair and set her up for the cut. Since her attention would be on her actions, not making eye contact, she decided to ask her a couple questions.

Not about Matt. That seemed like an invasion of his privacy. And fodder if Marley was considering matchmaking, which seemed likely.

"What made you become a guide?" she asked as she lined up her comb and scissors. The question seemed fairly safe, and she really was curious as to why someone would choose that as a profession, rather than a hobby, and marry someone who did it as well.

"I love the outdoors," Marley said simply. "Love how, on a tour, every day is different, even when we take multiple tours to the same place over time. It's never the same trip twice. I love the people. It's just a big thrill. I'm very blessed to be able to do what I love."

"Isn't it awfully dangerous?" Callie couldn't help the question. She couldn't quite wrap her mind around it.

Marley met her eyes in the mirror. Hers were a deep blue and very serious. "Yes, it can be. And there's a certain amount of risk in what we do, just by its nature. But we take every possible precaution and are never careless. Brice and Matt would fire anyone in a heartbeat if they were. But yeah, things can happen." She gave a little shrug. "Things can happen anywhere, even at home."

Callie understood that—look what had happened to her home! But what she didn't get was why people would put themselves in harm's way willingly. Even with all precautions taken, there was no guarantee it would all work out okay. She needed that guarantee for her boys. For herself.

"You should let Matt take you on a small trip," Marley said, and Callie nearly dropped her comb.

"Oh, I don't think so," she said with a laugh. "I've got little kids."

Marley frowned. "What does that have to do with it?"

"Well, I can't be irresponsible and take chances that might hurt them," Callie said bluntly. "They've lost their dad already. I can't—I can't take the chance of something happening to me, too."

Marley's face softened. "I know. I'm so sorry. Matt told me." She paused and Callie could see her weighing her next words. "But I guess I don't see how a small trip—maybe kayaking or something, or a bike ride, something local—is taking a serious chance with your life. You find your ability level and your comfort level and push just a little past them. You might surprise yourself."

Callie's comfort level was absolute zero with regards to risk. She'd lost too much to it already. "I don't know."

"Think about it." Marley met her eyes again. "I think it'd be good for him, too."

Callie thought over Marley's words the rest of the day. She really didn't have the time, inclination or money to take a trip, local or not. Yet despite her fear, there was a small part of her that remembered the girl she used to be. Before Jason had been killed in that fire rescuing a colleague. Before she got so afraid. She'd set that part of her aside, deciding at some point there was no room for that person anymore, now that she was a parent. A single parent. Fully responsible for two little boys.

She just wasn't sure she could afford to be that girl ever again.

Matt came home to an empty house, then remembered Callie was meeting the Marshalls to pick up the boys. It'd be loud and boisterous again soon enough. Funny how two little boys could seem like twice as many—or more.

Oddly enough, he was looking forward to it.

Even though he'd been, by nature of his job and temperament, someone who was fine being alone, he was starting to wonder if it was overrated. Sure, it was nice being responsible for only himself, and now Aldo, too. But yet—Matt wanted more, even though he hadn't realized it up till now.

He wasn't sure how much more. Or if it included a brown-eyed widow and her kids. All the noise and mess and uncertainty that came with being part of a family, being a parent. He didn't know if he had enough to offer them, especially being gone so often with his new job. He'd planned on staying more or less single. It seemed easier—no real risk for him in terms of his heart. In that way, he supposed he and Callie were similar. If he wanted to pick up and go, he could. Nothing was really tethering him down. He could hand in his notice—it was a month-to-month lease on this house—pack up and leave. Easy.

Except, despite everything, he was putting down roots. He'd made emotional commitments, to Callie and her boys. To Brice and Marley and the other employees. Matt liked having neighbors who waved when he pulled in his driveway, who said hello when he passed them while walking Aldo. This was a far cry from the stark, empty life he'd lived since Trina had left him.

Not because he'd loved her. No, because he'd thought she was right when she'd accused him of not being able to take care of anyone else other than himself. He'd accepted that life as normal, until Aldo had come into it. Now Callie and her boys—Jason's boys—had turned it upside down, and he was starting to see things differently.

Would Jason want Matt to be with Callie? They'd joked for years about his single state, about how he would most likely be single for-ever. It would be the height of irony if Matt and Callie did get together, after all. He didn't know if Jason would have approved or run him out of town.

There was no way to know. He didn't want to overstep his boundaries, but if there was even a tiny chance with Callie, should he take it?

Marley had come back and told him she'd got-ten her hair cut by Callie. She'd kept mum on the conversations they'd had, only to say she'd enjoyed it and loved the cut, and would be back. Matt hadn't seen any way to press, and was a little annoyed he'd wanted to know more about what Callie had said. Marley's smug look had been enough to keep his mouth shut. But she had suggested he put together a little day trip for Callie and him. While he'd been noncommittal at the time, now he wondered if she wasn't onto something. It might be a way to help Callie see how careful he really was. That it was okay for her to loosen up a little and maybe have some fun.

Because it mattered. He couldn't fully say why, but it did. He didn't want to see the shadows in her eyes when she talked about his work. He didn't want her to get upset looking at pictures. He wanted her to understand what drove him. Even if she ultimately decided it was too much for her, he wanted the chance.

Then he'd feel he'd done his best by Jason, done what he could to help her. The rest was up to her, when—or even if—she was ready.

"Mama!" Eli and Liam's excited shrieks brought tears to Callie's eyes. She opened her arms and pulled them close, feeling their warmth and smelling their sweet little-boy smells.

"Hi, guys," she said, her throat tight. She planted kisses on their faces. "I missed you."

Predictably, both wiggled loose after pressing against her for just a heartbeat longer than usual. She let them go and stood up.

Maureen pulled her in for a hug. "Good to see you, honey. Everything going okay?"

"As well as it can be, considering," Callie said, then added, "Just ready for it to be over. Matt's place is very nice, but I miss our house."

"I understand. Bill feels bad about the delay."

She shrugged. "I know, but it's not his fault. It'll get done. These things happen." She smiled. "Thanks so much for taking these guys. I know how much they love it."

Joe stepped up at that and gave her a hug, too, "It's mutual. Anytime, Callie. We love having them, and we'd love to have you, too. We retirees are happy for the distraction."

She was so grateful to have these two so close to her. They'd all leaned on each other in those dark days after Jason's death. It didn't replace having her own mother nearby, but was a pretty close second.

"So, would you like us to take them on the weekend? So you can get some more work done?" Maureen asked.

Callie hesitated. She hated to give the boys back again. Even for a couple days. She'd see how they all did at Matt's. "I'll let you know when I've got a better idea. Soon."

"You can call us on Saturday if need be," Joe said. "We know this is a tricky situation. Tell Matt hello for us. Love to see that boy again."

Shame trickled though her as she agreed to pass on the message. Not because it was the wrong thing to do, but because of the kisses. And the dreams. She felt even more guilty as she stood here with her in-laws.

Maureen and Joe hugged the boys, transferred gear, and Callie got them loaded up into her own van. Of course, the conversation centered on Matt and Aldo. While she'd expected the dog to be a prime topic of conversation, it unnerved her to have them so excited to see Matt, too. She didn't want them bonding, yet it seemed to have happened anyway. In fact, they were clearly past bonding and well on the way to hero-worshiping him.

She tried to shift the conversation to other topics, but it kept drifting back around to Matt. By the time she pulled into the driveway, she was sincerely wishing she had accepted Maureen's offer to stay with them, despite the inconvenience. So they'd be away from the man that held so much sway over her little boys after such a short time.

Matt was in the living room with Aldo when the kids burst in, Callie close on their heels. "I'm sorry," she said, meeting his humor-filled gaze. "They really missed Aldo. And you, too, apparently."

Matt opened his arms and hugged them both, and they squealed and laughed loudly. Then they set about petting the dog, who rolled right over on his back and practically groaned with pleasure.

Matt watched it all with amusement, but Callie couldn't help feeling concerned. When he turned to her, she said casually, "I'm going to get their things. Since they are clearly not going anywhere."

Matt chuckled and the warm sound filled her with longing. "I'd say you're right. Can I get it for you? You can stay here with them."

"Oh, no, it's just a couple bags. Oh, and a cooler. Maureen likes to cook."

His eyes lit up. "Awesome," he said. "She was always a great cook. I'll get that, then."

Since it was silly to argue, Callie walked outside and let him carry the cooler. Maureen had packed enough food for a week, but now that Callie thought about it, with two growing boys and a very fine adult male, it would probably last only a couple days.

Matt opened it and she left him sorting through the goodies with relish as she dropped the kids' bags in the room they all shared. She'd gotten some other stuff, a few toys and stuffed animals from the house, to help make it seem more homey. Matt had found a dresser a few days back. On that she'd put a lamp, plus clothes for all three of them in the drawers, and hung more up in the closet. Matt had bought drapes, as well, so the room felt a little less like a box. She appreciated all of it. Really.

But it wasn't home.

Though all that mattered to her was right here: her boys. There was some truth to the saying, "home is where the heart is," especially in a situation like this. *Matt matters, too.* She tried to ignore the unbidden little voice. Of course he did. But not enough to count as home.

The kids came tumbling in and she smiled when they fell on the mattress. Uh-oh. "This is mine, guys. You get the sleeping bags."

When they groaned, she pulled them both in for another hug. "No jumping, but you can lay on it." Though she knew she'd be reminding them again every five minutes not to jump, for now she was just happy they were with her.

Matt appeared in the doorway, looking far too good in faded jeans and an old sweatshirt. "What's all the noise in here? Sounds like someone's having a party."

"Matt!" Eli shrieked. "Come play with us. We got lotsa room!"

Matt's gaze glanced off hers. "I'm too big," he said easily, his tone belying the quick flash of longing she'd seen in his blue eyes. It was too intimate to invite him to snuggle with them, so she didn't offer. "I was just checking to make sure this room hadn't been taken over by wild and crazy animals." He grinned at them. "I see I was right to be worried."

The kids laughed and Callie had to smile. He pushed off the door frame and left the room, whistling.

It was a bit of a struggle to get them in bed that night, which wasn't a surprise. The joy of being back with Callie, plus the novelty of staying at Matt's, had them wound pretty tight. So she was fully prepared to read them an extra story, but was taken aback when Eli and Liam exchanged a look.

She glanced from one boy to the other. "Okay, guys, what is it?"

"We want Matt to read it to us tonight," Eli said, and Callie's heart seized. She swallowed hard, looking at their earnest little faces.

"I don't know if he can—" she started, but stopped when she saw both faces fall. "But I can go ask," she finished weakly. Both kids' faces split into huge smiles, and Callie got up to find Matt, trying not to feel betrayed. Which was silly. It was just a book.

No, it was more than that. It was another chink in the careful little world she'd created. A crack in their circle of three. She didn't know if there was a way to stop it from fracturing, now.

Matt looked up with a smile when she approached. She was momentarily tempted to flop down next to him and curl into his side. The urge threw her for a heartbeat, and Matt frowned and started to rise.

"They okay?" he asked, and she waved a hand.

"Just fine. They'd like you to read them a story." Her tone sounded casual enough. She hoped. "If you're up to it," she added.

He looked surprised. "I'd like that." He scanned her face, and apparently not seeing anything to dissuade him, asked, "Do they have one picked out?"

Callie nodded and he went down the hall. She fixed her gaze on the TV, but didn't see the program on the screen. This felt wrong. Wrong to let Matt read the kids a book? How silly was that?

Wrong because it was Matt and not Jason doing it?

Restless, Callie tucked her feet up under her. No, that wasn't the issue. It was more that it felt like a threat to her and her ability to keep them locked down and safe. Without a man in their lives who could leave them. And hurt them. Her boys didn't deserve that. Matt would be here, but for how long? He'd been in the army, moving around his entire adult life. He'd even said that life suited him. And he hadn't managed to convert being engaged into being married. Could he really be ready to settle down?

His low voice and the kids' laughter floated down the hall. She rubbed her hand between her eyes. On the other hand, perhaps she shouldn't overthink it; after all, it was just him reading them a story. And in a few days, a week maybe, they'd be back in their own home, able to return to normal. She could fix everything then, close that circle up and get them all back on track. She craved normal.

Except she was afraid after this whole experience with Matt—and Aldo—that normal had just made a major shift. And she wouldn't be able to put things back the way they had been.

Where would they be then?

CHAPTER ELEVEN

THE KIDS WERE HAPPY to go to Colleen's the next morning. Callie had intentionally scheduled her first appointment for a little later, so they could have some extra time in the morning. Lori completely understood. Matt was gone already and he'd taken Aldo with him, so it was just Callie and her boys, with no distractions. The kids clearly missed both of them, but Callie tried to overlook it. Pretend nothing had changed, it was all just temporary, and then maybe she could get things back to normal faster.

Except she wasn't fully sure what that was anymore. Their lives had shifted and she was afraid the old normal was a thing of the past.

But she enjoyed the time, and even made pancakes instead of the usual cold cereal. It was worth it to scrub maple syrup off their faces, and in Liam's case, out of his hair, just to see their smiles.

She took them to day care and they each hugged her before they headed into the play area. Colleen gave her a hug, too. "How are you holding up? When will your house be done? It was pretty busy over there for a while."

"Oh, we're fine," she said, wanting to sound as casual as possible, yet make absolutely sure Colleen knew there was nothing going on at Matt's. All without actually saying anything. It was tricky, and exhausting. She moved quickly to fill Colleen in on the current state of the repairs, and ended with, "I'm hoping to be back in there in a week or so." This was a bit optimistic.

To her credit, Colleen didn't argue or ask any difficult questions. Instead she smiled and said, "I hope so. It'll be wonderful to be back in your own space. Though I can't imagine living with Matt Bowden is any great hardship."

Sister, you have no idea. Callie didn't say the words, but wanted to. Instead she shrugged, opting not to touch the implication, and went with the truth. "He's been very patient. It can't be easy going from living alone your entire adult life to having all of us descend on him. Some days my little guys can make enough noise for two or three times as many kids."

Colleen laughed. "Don't I know it. That's a good point. Have a good day, Callie. We'll see you later."

Matt was busy unpacking a shipment of life jackets, trying to keep his thoughts off Callie and the complicated dance they were doing, when Brice came in. "You want to go for a ride? The trails at Torchfield Park are open. It'll be a little messy, and they won't have been cleared yet, but should be a good time. You want to give them a run? Marley will be fine here."

"Sure." It sounded way better than going round and round in his own head over things that went nowhere. After last night's reading session with the boys—and he'd seen the anguish in Callie's eyes when she'd told him they wanted him to read to them—he was thinking more and more about what exactly was going on here.

He still wasn't comfortable with this whole

idea, of him and his buddy's widow and all the physical and emotional stuff that was building between them. Still wasn't entirely sure what was the best thing to do.

But at the same time, whatever it was between them felt right. Even though she so clearly didn't want to feel it, too, and was fighting it as hard as she could. So he'd decided he wouldn't make any kind of move on it unless—or until—she wanted it, too.

He arranged a time with Brice, then ran home and got his bike and his gear, and dressed in old clothes for the wet and the mud. It was a warm enough day, but the trails would be an absolute mess. With that in mind, he threw in a couple old towels, as well.

He met Brice at the park. Aldo had stayed behind with Marley.

They unloaded their bikes and Matt noted they were the only ones parked here. Most other people were at work, or maybe weren't crazy enough to ride wet, muddy trails at the beginning of April. The two of them consulted the map carved on a wooden board at the head of the first trail. Matt hadn't ridden here before, as the bike trails had been added only recently, so it was a good idea to get a quick lay of the land.

"Ready?" Brice asked, buckling his helmet.

"Yep," he replied. They mounted their bikes and he let Brice take the lead. Matt stayed far enough back to avoid the majority of mud spraying up from his friend's wheels, but kicked up plenty of his own. His front and back would be filthy at the end of this ride.

It was a beautiful day. The lack of leaves on the trees meant the trails were clearly lit by the sun. There were all kind of downed branches, which at some point the county would remove from the easier trails for safety reasons, but would leave on the more advanced ones. The two of them hopped and swerved and went over all kinds of things, but on the way back, Brice's bike slid on a muddy curve and he went off into the brush at the side of the trail.

Matt pulled up next to him as his friend extricated himself from the pile, swearing a blue streak.

"You okay, buddy?" he asked as he got off his bike.

Brice shook his head, his jaw set hard. "Think I broke something."

His arm dangled at his side and Matt frowned. "Oh, man. All right. We're not too far from the trailhead. You okay to walk?"

Brice sent him a look that spoke volumes. Maybe he was hurt, but he was definitely no pansy.

Matt walked both bikes back—no easy feat in the mud—and got them both loaded into the back of his truck while Brice eased himself into the passenger seat. That was how he knew his friend was in pain—he didn't even try to drive his own truck.

"Straight to E.R. or stop for Marley first?" Matt asked as he backed out, then headed for town.

Brice let out a low hiss of pain when they hit a rut in the road. "Let her know to meet me there."

Matt fished his phone out and placed the call. Marley's reaction was what he expected from her—calm yet concerned. She said she'd be there right away.

Matt helped his friend out of the car and into the E.R. Both of them were beyond filthy, and later they'd no doubt laugh over the way the nurse frowned at the mud. Marley came in soon after Brice got checked in, and raised her brow.

"Wow, guys, you leave any mud out there?" She took Brice's free hand and patted his dirty knee. "I'd kiss you, but there's no clean place to do it."

He gave her a faint smile. "You're welcome."

Marley turned to Matt. "Aldo is in my car. Take Brice's keys to get him out, and I'll get them from you tomorrow."

"I will. Thanks. Get patched up quick so you can come back to work," he said to Brice, who lazily flipped him the bird with his good hand.

It was late, so Matt swung into a drive-through for a burger and fries, which he did not share with Aldo, despite his hangdog, begging looks.

"You're good," he told the dog, "but I'm immune."

Aldo let out a low woof and Matt laughed.

The house was lit up when he got home, and he wondered if he should have let Callie know he was going to be late. Well, no. That was one of those things he wasn't sure how to handle. If he had no feelings for her at all, he probably would have called and told her. But because he did, it was hard to know where the line was between okay and too much.

He climbed out with a groan. He was officially overthinking this. And he was sore. He'd used muscles today he hadn't used in a long time. Not as sore as Brice, after his header into the brush, though. That arm was going to hurt for a while.

Matt dropped his trash in the can in the garage and came in, Aldo behind him. Callie was at the sink doing dishes, and her eyes went wide at the sight of him. Too late, he remembered what a mess he was.

"Holy crap," she said. "What happened to you?"

"Bike ride," he answered. The kids came running at the sound of his voice, and he held up a hand to stop them as Callie made a diving catch and grabbed them. Better her soapy hands than his grubby ones.

"Whoa," Eli said.

"Dirty," Liam observed.

"Very," Callie said, amusement in her tone.

"You two have already had baths. You don't want to get all dirty and take another one, right?"

Both kids looked so horrified, Matt laughed. "Your mom's right. Let me get cleaned up, okay?"

She examined him and he opened his arms teasingly as her eyes widened. "Want a hug? The mud's all dry. It'll just brush off, probably." If not, she could join him in the shower. Now, that was an excellent idea. Best one he'd had all day.

She laughed, which he'd intended. "Thanks, but no thanks."

He came over for a drink of water and she inched back to let him pass. "Where did you go?"

"Torchfield Park. They've got mountain bike trails. We thought we'd break them in after a long winter of no biking. Instead, I think Brice got broken."

When he turned, he saw her face had gone pale. "Broken?"

Matt could have kicked himself for his poor choice of words. "He's okay, or will be," he assured her quickly. "He slipped on a curve and went down. Happens a lot, but this time he landed wrong in a pile of brush. Possibly a broken arm."

Her eyes were huge in her pale face and he realized she was spinning it up in her head. To him, this was a bike ride and the risks were part of it. Most of the time nothing happened. They got dirty, a little banged up, no big deal. This, while painful for Brice, was not a major problem in the general scheme of things. But to Callie it would signify the danger of what he chose to do in his everyday life.

Before he could speak, she did. "I don't get it. How can you call that fun? How can you put yourself out there like that? What if it had been worse and he'd broken his neck? What would Marley do?"

Callie's words came from a place of fear, he knew. But they rankled all the same. As if he and Brice just threw themselves out there with no regard for the consequences. He measured his response carefully. "We weren't careless, Callie. We knew it was slippery, knew either of us could fall. Like I said, it happens a lot. But it's usually only cuts and bruises, not broken bones or more serious injuries."

"But they can happen," she pressed.

He met her gaze head-on. It was critical he handled this right. Not sugarcoat it, but be sure he didn't make it more than it was. "Yes. They can. We take all precautions for each sport we're doing. We wear the proper safety equipment. In this case, we make sure the bikes are tuned up and ready to go. Wear helmets. Told Marley where we'd be. But we can't eliminate the risk from it completely. You can't do that. Not from anything, Callie. It's just not possible."

She opened her mouth to say something, then shut it and shook her head. "I hope Brice is all right," she said finally.

"He will be. Callie…" Matt moved closer and lifted her chin, saw the worry in her eyes and knew it was for more than his friend. "He'll be just fine. And he'll go back and do it again once he's healed."

She pulled back and Matt let her go. "I know. That's just it. I don't understand why."

He'd pushed her far enough. Maybe too far. But damn it, this wasn't within his control. Brice hadn't crashed on purpose. "I know you don't. I'm going to take a shower."

As he walked away, Matt felt her eyes on him and tried to pretend he didn't feel so helpless, when he wished he could help her understand. Why did her approval and understanding matter so much?

He wasn't sure he wanted the answer to that question. Because he was afraid it was that she was starting to mean far too much to him.

That night, after the boys were tucked in, Callie joined him in the living room. They usually got a half hour or so together before she retired to her air mattress and Matt sat out here alone. Tonight she folded herself up on the end of the couch, her hands clasped in her lap. "How's Brice?"

"Fine. Sore. Crashing isn't ever fun." Matt watched her carefully for a reaction.

"I'm glad he's okay," she said, then hesitated. "Matt. Why did you leave the army?"

She couldn't have caught him more off guard if she'd punched him. When he didn't say anything, she continued, "Jason always said how well it suited you as a career. But yet, you're here."

He took a deep breath. Instinct told him to deflect her question, to push it away. But it was a legitimate query. Plus Callie was looking at him, and while there was sympathy in her gaze, there was no pity. He rubbed his hand over his face. The words were simple, but so damn hard to get out.

"We saw a lot over there," he said finally. "I don't know that you ever get used to it, exactly, but you kind of learn to live with it. To separate yourself from the job. Or I did, anyway. But at the end…" He took a deep breath, felt a rattle in his lungs. He never talked about this. Ever. But he needed to tell her.

She didn't move, just sat and waited, her expression soft and open. So the words eventually came. "At the end of my tour—well, I had about five weeks left, which is still a long time in a place like that. But we'd befriended some kids. You know, on the street. Some had families, some didn't. One boy sort of belonged to Aldo. Fahran. Until one day he was walking past a grocery store and a suicide bomber detonated his explosives." Matt's voice broke on the words. So many had died that day. Mostly women and children, many kids younger than Fahran.

Callie sucked in a breath and Matt saw the horror in her eyes. But he kept talking. The words wouldn't stop now. "I wasn't that far away, but I couldn't get there in time. He died before he got any help. I didn't know him that well, but somehow it just hit me. Really hard. I wouldn't say I cracked, exactly, but I just couldn't do it anymore. All that senseless dying. I'd told him to be careful. He laughed and waved, and took off like every other time."

Matt laughed, but there was no humor in it. "It wasn't my first time in the combat zone. Wasn't the first time I'd seen something like that. But it was the last straw."

Callie's voice was soft. "So you saved Aldo instead."

Matt fiddled with the TV remote in his hands. It was a small thing to have done, almost inconsequential in the scheme of things. "Yeah." He shrugged. "It's not really anything. It didn't solve any problems, bring anyone back. Didn't save Fahran."

"Don't say that. Sure, it's something," she said, and her tone was fierce. Matt glanced up in surprise. "It's everything. You do what you can, Matt. Look at Aldo. He's so much better off now."

The dog nudged Matt's hand with his head. Aldo's eyes were soulful, and Matt wondered if his buddy understood what was going on here. He stroked the dog's head gently. "He is. He's my friend. But I still wish—" He cut himself off. Wishing he'd detained the boy for ten extra minutes didn't do any good. Who could say it would have made a difference?

Callie moved over and rested her hand on his thigh. "I know you do. But you can't know what's going to happen all the time. You can't blame yourself. That's not fair."

He reached out and touched her hair. Her eyes were luminous, and all he wanted to do was lose himself in her. "I'm working on it." That was all he could say before he leaned in and kissed her. As soon as his mouth touched hers, he knew.

He was lost.

Callie couldn't get the whole thing with Matt out of her head the next day. She really didn't understand how he could put himself in danger like that, just for kicks. Yes, it was his job, but it was still for fun. He chose to do what he did. The result was he would put himself at risk each time he went on one of those tours. Brice had gotten hurt, and that hit just a touch too close to home.

Of course, this wasn't Afghanistan. After being in a war zone, dealing with what he had, maybe this stuff seemed like child's play to Matt. Her heart ached for him, for the loss that had finally broken him. He'd seen enough death and destruction to last him for several lifetimes, she knew. He carried it with him, and it was symbolized in Aldo. Matt couldn't save them all, but he could save this one lonely, scared, injured dog.

Running rapids and riding trails seemed to pale in comparison. No wonder he couldn't see where she was coming from. So they were at an impasse of sorts, and Callie didn't know how to get past it. If it was possible to do so or if she even wanted to. Did she want him around her boys if he made those kinds of decisions on a day-to-day basis?

Because she was facing the possibility that she might have feelings for Matt—and since she'd already kissed him three times, including last night's short and sweet one, she couldn't deny that to herself any longer. Callie sat in the bedroom of her empty house. Regardless of how this situation with Matt turned out, it was time to take off her rings. She'd come over here to do it, because she needed to be alone. This was a moment she'd been dreading, in a way, but she knew it was time. Probably past time, really. With a deep breath, she slid her rings off and turned them in the late afternoon sunlight that streamed through the window. They represented so much love and joy and potential, pain and sorrow and loss. But with her growing feelings for Matt—whatever they were, whatever she did with them, they weren't going away—she couldn't justify wearing the rings any longer. It was wrong to hide behind Jason's memory, just because she was afraid of what the future might have in store for her.

He wouldn't have understood that. He'd always gone full bore after what he wanted, her included.

The diamond winked in the light and she smiled a little, remembering how thrilled she'd been when Jason had proposed. And she wouldn't have traded those years for anything. Even knowing how it might end, she'd jumped in with both feet and embraced their lives together. She'd been aware of the dangers. Jason had been up front about his job from the beginning. Had she simply been young and foolish, to think it wouldn't go the way it had? Or was it an innate part of her personality that she was now suppressing?

When had she lost that ability? When she'd lost Jason, that part of her had been buried under the stress and grief. But was it completely obliterated? If so, she knew there was no way to make it work with Matt.

She turned the rings around again. Callie had Jason's wedding ring, too. Maybe she could have them melted down and made into some kind of charm? Representative of her marriage and loss and love. Somehow, if things progressed with Matt, she knew he wouldn't mind that. It seemed fitting.

She didn't know yet if she was ready to take that step forward with Matt. If she ever would be. She had a lot to figure out when it came to him and his choices and her comfort zones. For now, removing the rings was as big a step as she could handle.

She padded across the floor and opened her jewelry box. Jason's ring lay in there, and she pulled it out, feeling its weight. He hadn't worn it on the job, but always had it on when he wasn't working. She dropped it in her palm with her own rings and closed her fingers over them, feeling the bite of the diamond and the cool metal of Jason's ring. She kissed her closed hand and put all the rings in the box together.

She stood for a moment, feeling a little sad, sure, but as if she'd done the right thing by taking them off. Knowing it was time—however it worked out, or didn't, with Matt. She touched the box and left the room. After Jason's death, people had told her life went on. Callie hadn't believed them at the time, but they were right.

She left her little house to walk over to Colleen's and get the boys. Her newly naked hand felt exposed, and she was sure she'd keep feeling for the rings for a while. But she'd adjust.

Now she just had to figure out what to do about

Matt. She didn't know if she could fully accept what he did for a living, yet it wasn't fair to ask him to change because of her issues.

CHAPTER TWELVE

"MOM! LOOK!" ELI called out later that evening as she got home from a trip to the store. It took her a full second to realize his voice was coming from near the middle of the medium-size maple tree in Matt's side yard. Her heart seized and she gasped. She was out of her van so fast she didn't even get the keys out of the ignition.

"Eli Marshall! Get down from there this instant!" Matt was there, right there, but Eli was *in the tree*. If he fell, he could get hurt. How could Matt let him do that? All her decisions to be rational about Matt and his lifestyle went out the window as soon as she spotted her baby in a tree. A tree!

Eli pushed his lower lip out, the look of delight gone, replaced with mutiny. "No. I don't wanna come down. You never let me climb a tree."

"Callie—" Matt started, but she cut him off. She couldn't take her eyes off her boy in the tree.

"I don't let you climb trees because it isn't safe, Eli. That's a very good reason." Without removing her eyes from her son, she said to Matt, "Get him down. Now." The fury, the fear—part of her knew it was out of proportion, since Eli was only a few feet off the ground. But Matt knew how she felt about risks, and this was a huge one *he'd taken with her child*.

She thought she was going to be sick. "Eli—"

"Come here, Eli," Matt said calmly, reaching for the boy, who actually scrambled even higher out of reach. The branches creaked and bowed, but held him. Callie gasped and her hands flew to her mouth. Eli had always been a monkey. She and Jason had been fishing him off high ground since he'd figured out how to climb. How had she forgotten that?

"Eli," she cried. "Come down from there. Now!"

Matt never took his eyes off Eli, but spoke to Callie, his voice low and measured, which infuriated her more. How could he be so calm when she was so freaked out? "You're not help-ing, Callie."

Oh. She sucked in a breath sharply. Of course, he was probably right, but it stung to hear it. She couldn't help this panic, this fear. *What if something happened? What if Eli got hurt?* She'd never be able to live with herself. She'd been right to protect them from this kind of thing. From people who allowed it.

She crossed her arms over her chest and stood, eyes burning with unshed tears, as Eli sent her angry looks. Matt never glanced her way, but kept his gaze on her boy, his voice low and calm and firm. Eli relented finally, and Callie thought she'd collapse with relief when he let Matt reach up and pluck him from the tree.

"Here, buddy, you can go to your mom," Matt said, and tried to set the boy on the ground. But Eli shook his head as Callie reached for him. He wrapped his arms and legs around Matt and hung on.

"Wanna stay with you," he mumbled, and sent his mom a fierce look. She sucked in a gasp, his rejection stinging like a slap. Matt touched the back of Eli's head, sent her an apologetic look and inclined his head toward the house. Callie stood frozen in the front yard as the big man carried her angry little boy inside. He looked like a dad.

That fueled her anger. He wasn't their dad. He'd said he would watch them, keep them safe for twenty minutes, and instead he'd let Eli climb a tree. A tree! Who let a five-year-old climb a tree?

Realizing how foolish she looked standing in the yard with her mouth open, she snapped it shut, retrieved her keys from her van and marched in after them. Eli was in the bathroom washing up, if the sounds from that direction were any indication. Matt was in the kitchen, leaning on the counter, his face grim.

"We need to talk," he said.

All she could do was stare at him, her anger, already simmering, bubbling up just below the surface. His tone implied the problem lay with her. He couldn't have been more wrong. "Yeah, you're right, we do. But first I'm going to talk to my kid. I'll deal with you later."

She turned and walked away before he could say anything.

* * *

Eli was not contrite. Callie was somewhat be-
mused by this stubborn side of her son, which occasionally reared its head. But today was the first
time she'd seen it for an extended period of time.

She tried again. "Honey, it's dangerous to climb
trees. You can get hurt."

Eli jutted out his chin. "But I didn't."

That's not the point, Callie wanted to scream.
Instead, she sighed. "No. But if you ever do it
again, Eli, I will take away your TV and computer privileges."

He frowned at her. "Why can't I? I like to
climb."

No argument from her on that front. "I know.
But climbing trees isn't safe. You can fall. You
might get up too high. Sometimes branches are
dead, and you can't tell until you put your weight
on one and it breaks. I'm trying to make sure you
stay safe, honey."

Eli crossed his arms over his chest. "Matt said
that tree was okay. He said I could go a little way
up. And he was right there."

Oh, my. She exhaled slowly, fully aware of the

minefields in that statement. Not to mention Eli had gone more than "a little way up." She tried again. "I know he did. But Matt was wrong to let you climb the tree. He's not a parent. He didn't ask me first."

Did he go against her wishes? Or did he truly think there was no harm in letting Eli climb up a little way? Had she not been clear enough on her feelings about her kids being exposed to things that could hurt them?

"You weren't here," Eli pointed out.

"No," she agreed. "But he should have waited and asked me." She would have said no, and dealt with the meltdown from Eli, which would have been almost preferable to this stubbornness.

He set his jaw and glanced away. He looked just like a miniature copy of his dad in that moment and Callie wanted to cry. "Why can't Matt be my dad?"

Of all the things he could have said, that wasn't one she'd ever considered. She gripped her hands together in her lap so tightly she thought she'd crack her fingers. This conversation had just taken a serious left turn. "Well, because you have a dad."

"He's not here. But I know if he was he'd let me climb a tree." Eli's face was set in hard lines.

The thing was, Eli was probably right. The thought made Callie feel even worse about her reaction, but Jason wasn't here because of his dangerous job. "I know your dad isn't here anymore, but we're fine, Eli, with just the three of us."

He just looked at her and her heart sank a little. Of course he wanted a dad. Every kid deserved to have both parents. It killed her she couldn't give this one thing to her child. "Can I go now?"

She sat back with a sigh. She wasn't really getting anywhere with this, anyway. She'd not convinced him about the danger of climbing trees, and he'd thrown her for a loop with the wanting-Matt-for-a-dad comment. "Sure."

He slid off the chair and stomped down the hall to where Liam was playing with cars. Callie leaned forward and rested her elbows on her knees, her face in her hands. She wanted to scream. Or cry. Or both. How had that gone so badly? Of course Eli couldn't understand her concern. He was a kid. But Matt—what he'd done was wrong. And she hoped like crazy he hadn't just overheard Eli say he wanted him for a dad. She'd been crazy to think she could let Matt into their lives. That was just too much, and under-scored what she already knew—that it was time to get out of here if she'd have any hope of sal-vaging her little family and getting it back under her own control. She was the only one who could keep them safe. Matt had just proved that.

She should thank him for stopping this before she got in any deeper.

Matt went out in the garage, pulling the door shut quietly behind him, his mind reeling. Eli's words ricocheted in his head. *Why can't Matt be my dad?*

Why not? There were a hundred reasons, too many to count. He wasn't really father material. Uncle material, sure. He bet he could do uncle pretty well. Not be fully responsible for any of them, but still be in their lives. Help when they needed it, but not step in to fill that crucial father role. Today, when all he'd done was let Eli climb a few feet off the ground in a great climbing tree, he'd proved he wasn't parent material in Callie's eyes.

Plus, they were Jason's kids. How could he want to step in and take his friend's place? Did he want to? If they weren't Jason's, would the answer be different?

It didn't matter now. Matt definitely wanted things from Callie he had no business wanting. But replacing Jason wasn't one of them. That was for damn sure.

Matt heard the door from the kitchen open, and when he turned to look, he saw Callie standing there, her beautiful face set in angry lines. His heart sank as he rested one hip on the workbench he'd been staring at. This wasn't going to go well.

"I don't let them do things like climb trees," she said bluntly. "I'd appreciate it if you wouldn't, either."

"I'm sorry, Callie," he said. "I won't let him do it again." Not that he'd have the chance. He'd bet she was gearing up to run even as she stood there. She wasn't going to give him a chance to be a dad to them, even if he wanted it. Even if the kids wanted it.

"Thank you," she said stiffly, and turned to go inside.

He cleared his throat. He might as well get it all out, if he'd lost her anyway. "But I think you're wrong."

She froze, her hand on the knob. She turned back around, her expression incredulous. "What did you say?"

He met her gaze. He was in this now, for better or worse. "I think you're taking this too far. You're a great mom. But your reaction to Eli climbing a little way up a tree today was much too strong. You scared him."

"As I should have," she pointed out, her tone cold. "He's not supposed to do that kind of thing. He could get hurt." Her expression clearly said this wasn't something she should have to explain.

Matt forged on. "But he didn't, Callie. That's my point. I shouldn't have let him do it without asking you, and I am sorry for that. But I was right there. He's a curious, active kid. But you won't let him be either. Why is that?"

Shock crossed her face as she shook her head. "I'm keeping him safe," she said. "I'm doing my job as a parent. I'm not trying to stifle him. Or hurt him."

Matt shook his head. She needed to see exactly what she was doing. "Of course you're not. But you scared him today. He was having a great time, proud of himself and excited to show you what he'd done, all by himself, and you freaked out."

She tipped her chin up and her eyes flashed with anger. "Of course I did. I hope he got scared and won't do it again. I can't let him take risks like that, Matt. I wouldn't be a good mom if I let him get hurt. And if he's mad for a while, well, he'll get over it."

Here was a sticking point for Matt. He moved toward her and she stood her ground on the steps. "How are you a bad mom if he does get hurt, Callie? He's a kid. They get things like bumps and bruises and the occasional broken bone. Kids fall off bikes and get hit by baseballs and trip over toys on the floor in their rooms. Getting banged up is part of growing up. It's not always under your control. Accidents happen, kids occasionally get hurt, and then they get better again and go back for more." He stopped in front of her and her position on the step put her at eye level with him. In hers, he saw the anger, the fear. The confusion.

She looked away and crossed her arms firmly over her chest. He continued, "But if you overreact to it, you make it more than it needs to be. It's fine to be upset he was in the tree. It's fine to be concerned about his safety. You have every right to be both of those. But maybe you need to make sure you don't cross the line and push him into doing this stuff on purpose."

Overreacted? Not really. True, she'd been so focused on what could have happened that she hadn't really looked at what was actually happening. Matt had been right there, and Eli hadn't been very high up, true. But it'd been too high for her, and she'd been unable to stop the huge swell of panic that had overtaken her.

So no, it wasn't an overreaction.

But right now she was angry and hurt and feeling a little betrayed by all of them. The picture of Matt carrying Eli flashed in her mind's eye. Her angry little boy snuggled in those big, strong arms. As if they'd formed a unit and cut her out. It made her panicky. Things were changing too rapidly and she couldn't seem to stop any of it. Slow any of it down. What was wrong with doing what you had to, whatever it took, to keep the people you loved safe? Even if it made them unhappy in the short run, it was for their own good. Someday they'd understand.

"He won't do any of it if I can help it," she said flatly, and turned to go inside, not bothering to see if Matt followed her or not. His refusal to see her side of it made her a little queasy. Her mom, her friends, all of them said the same thing, and while maybe part of her saw their point, a larger part wasn't so sure. And until she knew, she couldn't sort it out.

She turned back around, unable to resist making one last point, since it was all over, anyway. "And this is rich, coming from you. You who take all these dangerous chances for a living. Matt, I don't want my boys exposed to this stuff. Any of it. It's not—it's not okay with me."

Anger flashed in his eyes. "How is that going to work out? Are you ever going to let them ride a bike, Callie? A skateboard? Play sports?" He must have read the answer on her face because he added, "You can't control everything about their lives. You can't stop them from ever getting hurt. That's my whole point. Don't you think they should see how to handle this sort of thing responsibly?"

"How is it responsible to let a little kid climb a tree? Or to ride a bike in the mud when you know what can happen?" she hissed back. "Or go white-water rafting? How is it responsible to put yourself on the line like that? In danger? It's no way to be a role model to little boys."

Her own words echoed hollowly in her head. Was that really how she saw him? As someone who, willy-nilly, took risks, with no regard to the consequences? Or was it an excuse, a way to put distance between herself and her feelings? Already, to Eli, Matt was a hero. A fatherlike figure. Was she too late to reverse this? She'd gotten involved without meaning to, and look where they'd ended up.

His face was a mask. There was no emotion on it as he stared at her. "How are you going to explain Jason to them when they're older?" he asked. "Sugarcoat what he did? How he died? How can you do that? There was far more risk in his job than there is in mine."

She sucked in a sharp breath. Not that long ago she'd been comparing them, too. "It's not the same," she said stiffly, and Matt shook his head.

He moved closer, close enough she could have kissed him if she was brave enough. The fact she wanted to kiss him, take all this pain and anger and spin it out into something beautiful, caught her off guard, and she almost flinched away from him.

His tone was hard. "This isn't about me. It's not even about Jason. It's about you, and how you are too scared to live your life the way you should in case something goes wrong. It's about you trying to control and micromanage those boys to pieces. Already both are showing signs of their daddy's personality. Are you going to shut that down in them? How do you think you can do that, without them resenting the hell out of you for it?"

"I'm going to protect them!" she shouted. "That's what mothers do. Protect their kids from harm and danger. That is what I'm doing. And you have no right to tell me I'm wrong. No right at all." Her eyes blazed as she poked him in the chest with her finger.

His eyes narrowed as he caught her left hand. He ran the rough pad of his thumb over the place her rings had been. He looked at her, shock and regret on his face, and she wished with her whole heart she'd left them on, left up that last barrier, because she'd opened herself to emotional destruction. For a moment, there was a flash of strong feeling on his face, then the hard mask was back. He dropped her hand and she felt the loss of contact keenly.

"You're right," he said flatly. "I don't have the right to tell you what to do. But you don't have the right to impose your fears on your kids, either. That's exactly what you're doing. And you refuse to see it." He moved around her into the house, not touching her, not making eye contact. Her skin prickled in that way it did when he was near, like electricity dancing over her skin. She

suppressed the unwelcome little shiver that followed the feeling. Even now, even angry as she
was at him, she still responded to him. It was infuriating. Aldo, who'd been waiting on the other
side of the door, apparently sensed the tension
flowing between them, because he gave a little
whine and nudged her hand, then padded after
Matt.

She stood there in the doorway and watched
them go, pain and fury mingling with something
else, a suspicion that she was on the verge of
ruining something hard-won and precious. She
fought down the tears and dropped her head on
her hands. She'd get out of here tomorrow. She'd
call Bill to be sure her place was livable enough,
with the tarp on the roof, and if so, they'd go
home. If not, they'd go to Maureen and Joe's,
despite the inconvenience. Callie couldn't stay
here any longer.

She got herself under control and entered the
house quietly. With nowhere else to go, she went
to sit on the couch, noting that Matt's bedroom
door was closed. Part of her wanted to chase him,
but she knew she was right to take this stand.

She was right to protect her kids at any cost. There was no doubt there. They could get hurt in too many ways from too many things, and they needed her to stand between them and those things. That's all she was doing. She wasn't wrong. Matt didn't understand, because he hadn't ever had the kind of loss she had. The point was, while they were so small she could control what they were exposed to, and she would.

Laughter from the rear bedroom made her shut her eyes and sit back on the couch. She pressed her fingers between her eyebrows and fought the tears. She was doing what she thought was best for her children by keeping them safe. It wasn't always going to be pretty, and they wouldn't always like it, but that was part of parenting. And doing it alone was that much harder. There was no one to lean on, to back her up.

Matt's face flashed in her mind. She winced. He hadn't backed her up. He'd encouraged her son to do something dangerous, and didn't seem to fully understand her justification for being so upset. He'd argued that it was just what kids did. That they got hurt all the time.

Well, okay, maybe. But not her kids. Not as long as she had any say.

But for how long would she have that say? They'd grow up all too quickly and, as Matt had warned, resent her bitterly for suppressing their adventurous sides....

CHAPTER THIRTEEN

MATT FOUND HIMSELF at work the next day with a grumpy Brice and a hovering Marley.

Brice's arm was wrapped and splinted. "He wouldn't stay home," Marley said, concern and annoyance layered in her tone.

"What am I going to do at home? I stayed home yesterday," he said irritably, and she lifted an eyebrow.

"Take it easy?" she suggested in a sugar-sweet tone that made Matt think this wasn't the first time they'd had this particular conversation. Or even the second. When Brice didn't answer, only scowled, she threw her arms up. "Men are such babies. I'm going for coffee."

She grabbed her purse and swept out the door. Amused, Matt turned to study his friend. "Maybe I should go back home. Give you guys some space to fight."

Brice scowled. "It's a broken arm. Not a huge deal. Just wait till you get hooked into this whole thing."

Matt chose to misunderstand his friend's meaning. He wasn't getting hooked into anything, not after his blowup with Callie. "I don't plan on falling off my bike and breaking any bones."

"Hah." Brice shook his head. "That's not what I meant and you know it. I'm talking about Callie."

"I'm not," he said, keeping his tone mild even as he thought of her anger and fear and all the issues that stood between them. "There's nothing that's going to happen there." Yet she'd taken off her rings. Why? Did it mean she had feelings for him? He knew her well enough to know she wouldn't have removed them without a great deal of thought.

"Why not?"

Matt shoved his hands in his pockets. Where did he begin? There were so many reasons, it was impossible to know which one was the deal breaker.

"She isn't interested in a guy who takes risks for a living," he said finally, because that summed it up the best. "And I can't do anything else. So—" he shrugged as if it didn't matter, as if it wasn't eating him up inside that she'd taken her rings off "—that's that."

"That's crazy," Brice said flatly.

"It is what it is," Matt said, trying to pretend he wasn't torn up by the thought of Callie not being in his life. Of losing the boys. Not just because of his connection to Jason, although that was part of it. But because he really and truly liked all of them, liked Callie.

Maybe far more than that, but going there was too painful. So he wouldn't even try. He'd worked hard to keep his heart out of this. He strongly suspected he'd failed miserably and that was why this hurt so damn bad.

Brice set his casted arm on the table with a thump and a wince. "So that's it? You'll just let her walk away?"

Since his friend wasn't going to drop it, Matt gave in. "I don't see any other choice. I let Eli climb a tree and she went crazy. You fell off your bike and it just cemented in how dangerous my life is. All the precautions, all the safety equip-

ment in the world isn't enough." Because it hadn't
saved Jason. And she was so terrified of something happening she couldn't control, she'd gone
too far the opposite way. Matt got that. Really,
he did. "She can't handle any kind of risk. She
tries to control every possible thing, and that's
just not rational." Bottom line, it wasn't any way
to have a relationship. She'd be in a constant state
of fear, and he didn't want that. For any of them,
but especially the boys.

"I know you don't want my advice. But I'm giving it to you anyway. Don't let her get away. She
needs you, Matt. Those kids need you. I almost
let Marley go, remember?" Brice shook his head.
"I can't even imagine being so stupid. But I was."

Matt stared at the ceiling. "This isn't the same.
I don't know how to make her see that what she's
doing is making things harder for herself and the
boys. She's not even speaking to me and we live
in the same house." For now. It wouldn't shock
him to find she'd moved out by the end of the
day. She'd probably called Bill last night to see
if her place was livable. If it wasn't, she'd prob-

ably go to Maureen and Joe's. Either way, she'd run. Matt had totally blown it.

Brice opened his mouth to speak, and he shook his head. "There's nothing to say. Thanks, though. I appreciate the ear."

"Don't be an idiot," Brice declared, and when Matt looked at him sharply he saw his friend was serious. "It had to be said. You've got all the signs of being one. So don't do it."

"Don't do what?" Marley asked as she came through the door, cardboard coffee-holder in hand. Matt shook his head, but Brice said, "Be stupid about Callie."

Marley removed one of the cups from the holder and handed it to her husband, then another, which she handed to Matt. "Are you in danger of being stupid about her?"

He took the cup. "No."

"Yes," countered Brice. Marley nodded.

"Let me see if I've got this straight. You're in love with her, but hiding your feelings behind her husband. She's scared, but she has reason to be." Marley took a sip of her coffee and shrugged at

Matt's shock. "You're so easy to read. What are you going to do about it?"

It took him a second to sort through everything she'd said. "I'm not hiding behind Jason." Actually, he'd intended to deny he was in love with Callie. Why hadn't he?

"Aren't you?" Marley's eyes were implacable. Matt sent a *save me* look to Brice, who just shook his head, a small grin on his face. She continued on. "You're trying to filter all this through Jason. What would he want? What would he want you to do? Would he be okay with this relationship? But what matters is, what does Callie want? What do you want? This relationship is about you and her, not her and Jason, or you and Jason."

"It doesn't matter. I'm not in love with her," Matt said shortly, and turned to walk away. What was Marley talking about, hiding behind Jason? He wasn't doing that. There was no way to make it work, even if they wanted to—and Callie had been clear she didn't want that. Even though she'd taken her rings off, it wasn't enough to overcome the fact that he'd wrecked the situation by being cavalier with Eli's safety, as she saw it.

"Oh, yes you are," he heard Marley say, but her tone wasn't smug this time. It was sad. Brice said something, but Matt didn't catch it as he closed his office door. He sank down behind the desk and stared at the computer, not seeing it. Not seeing anything but Callie's stricken face when she'd spotted Eli in the tree. Or when she'd finally decided what Matt did for a living made him too reckless and dangerous, and he wasn't the man for her.

Seeing her bare ring finger.

He shut his eyes and dropped his head into his hands. Funny how he hadn't been even remotely this torn up when his fiancée had dumped him. He'd been almost relieved then. Now, he felt actual physical pain over a loss of someone—three someones, to be exact—he'd never had any kind of claim to in the first place.

"You're moving out today?" Lori asked. She arched a brow. "Hmm. What happened?"

"Nothing," Callie said. The lie was ash on her tongue. "It's just time. I'd like to get it done before he comes home." She'd managed to avoid him this morning—or rather, he'd avoided her. He'd been gone before she'd gotten up. She'd heard him, but decided not to face him.

Call her a coward. She would fully own up to that.

Lori examined her. "The house is ready? I thought the roof and attic still needed work?"

Callie examined her station, rearranging things that were perfectly fine where they were. "Turns out I can live with that."

Lori made a little noise and Callie met her eyes, finally. "It's just time, Lori." When her friend stayed quiet, she added, "We disagree over some very key things." The memory made her heart hurt. "I don't think it's a good idea to have him around the boys."

"What?" Lori drew back. "Why not?"

She wondered how to explain this. Straightforward seemed the best option. "He takes unnecessary chances."

"Okay," her friend said carefully. "Define unnecessary."

Callie frowned. She shouldn't have to. It was clear to her. "Look at him, Lori. The bikes, where his friend got hurt. The white-water rafting. He let Eli climb a tree. He does all these things that are dangerous, and that's a bad example for the boys."

Understanding lit Lori's eyes. "Does he ignore the safety precautions?"

Callie drew back. Lori was supposed to be on her side. "I—well, no. Not that I know of. But the point is those things aren't entirely safe." Why was this clear only to her?

"Neither is driving your van every day," Lori pointed out. "But you buckle those boys in their seats and take them anyway, right? What about your house? The tree fell on it and you could all have been inside. The point is, everything, every day, carries risk. You can't hide from it." Her voice softened. "And I know how hard you've tried, honey."

Tears pricked Callie's eyes. "Wanting my kids to be safe isn't hiding," she pointed out, feeling a little betrayed by Lori's words. "It's being responsible."

"Yes," she agreed. "It is. And you are very responsible. But you are also so wrapped up in fear that you've taken it way too far. You won't let anyone in, and you won't let the kids out. What happened to Jason was awful," she said, her voice softer. "No one blames you for being gun-shy. No one. But you've got to move past the fear. Jason wouldn't want this. He loved his job and wouldn't have changed it, even knowing what might happen. He'd want you guys to live your lives to the fullest. That may or may not include having another man in your life, Callie—only time will tell. But sheltering your boys like you do only hurts them in the long run. Not to mention, to the kids, it makes anything you define as risky behavior even more attractive."

Callie stood perfectly still. Lori's words echoed Matt's, and as it had then, the truth of them unwittingly worked its way in. "I don't know how anymore." The admission was wrenching. She didn't. She hadn't meant to lock them up in a tower away from the world. She'd only meant to be sure they were safe, and as time went on, and she'd focused so much on the risks Jason had taken, on the risks of his profession, she'd simply lost sight of the bigger picture.

But there were more risks in life than just the physical kind. The emotional ones were just as daunting. She wasn't sure she could open up like that, and take those chances again, if the outcome might be devastation.

Then again, what if it wasn't? There was no way to know. And living in fear wasn't honoring the memory of her incredibly brave husband.

"You're not wearing your rings," Lori said suddenly. She lifted her eyes, and Callie saw the emotion in her friend's gaze. "Callie. You took them off."

Callie looked down at her bare hand, still feeling the loss. She'd gotten so used to them, not wearing them felt weird, but not wrong. "I decided it was time." She stood behind that decision, even though things hadn't worked out with Matt.

"Oh, honey." Lori shook her head. "Does Matt know you are in love with him?"

Callie sucked in a breath as the words pinged around in her head. *In. Love. With. Matt.* "I'm not." Could she be? After so long without Jason, thinking there was nothing more for her, had she gone and fallen in love with Matt?

Of course not. He was all wrong for her.

She lifted her eyes to Lori's and saw understanding there. "You've got some things to figure out," her friend said quietly. "But running away won't change any of it."

Callie packed up their stuff quickly and efficiently, trying not to hear Lori's words over and over on a loop in her brain. *In love with Matt.* Not possible.

She forced her attention back to the task at hand. It was going to take a couple trips—the pans were unwieldy—but she'd get it all out of here in less than an hour. She was tempted to leave the key on the table, but that was the ultimate cowardly move, and while she was definitely a coward, she at least owed him the face-to-face key return after he'd put them up for so long.

She turned up the heat at her place, vacuumed up the construction dust and set up the boys' bedroom. The tidying kept her busy and her mind off the hard kernel of pain in her chest that seemed to expand every time she thought of Matt.

Which happened with every other breath.

She hauled all her stuff home and dumped it in the newly cleaned living room. She had to head back to work, so there was no time to unpack anything, but she'd get to it when she got home after work.

The kids wouldn't be happy, but this was for their own good, she reminded herself as she drove to the salon. Not that Matt would ever hurt them, but he wasn't a good role model. They'd see him reveling in dangerous activities and would want to do the same. She couldn't have that. They had to come first.

But the thoughts were hollow. Somehow, she wasn't convinced anymore. Her plan had been so simple—keep them safe and sheltered, and keep her own heart safe and sheltered, too. Just navigate as a small family through their childhoods, until they were old enough to take care of themselves. It seemed simple enough.

Well, except life wasn't simple, and if anyone knew that, it was Callie. She'd clung to her plan—still did, to some extent—because it let her think she had some control over things she really didn't.

Such as her kids' hearts. And, apparently, her own.

Tears stung her eyes. It didn't really matter now. She'd made her choice to go it alone, and she'd make it work, but with the understanding that she'd been too simplistic. Her eyes were open now.

But something was missing. Something that had been within her grasp. Not what she'd had with Jason—not exactly. No, this was different. Something had been growing, and it'd been cut off the last couple of days when she'd realized she couldn't take Matt as he was.

And she couldn't change him. She wouldn't ask; it wasn't fair. That wasn't how it worked.

"Wait, Mom, why are we going here?" Eli asked that evening, suspicion lacing his voice as they walked up the steps to their house. Liam dragged his feet so hard Callie had to pick him up and carry him.

"Because there's no reason to stay over at Matt's anymore," she said, forcing cheer into her voice. "Ours is almost ready and our house misses us. Don't you guys miss your room? Your own beds and all your toys?" She was playing the bribe card, no doubt about it. Sad to say, she wasn't above it if it would smooth the transition.

"Yeah," Eli said. "But I wanna go to Matt's. Why can't we take all our stuff there?"

Callie's heart froze. She should have known they'd get attached to him. Now they were getting hurt. Just as she'd known they would.

"Because this is our house," she said firmly. "We live here. You can visit Matt and Aldo." She hoped. "If they're not too busy," she added.

Liam started to cry, and Eli wasn't far behind. Callie wanted to weep right with them, but it wasn't an option. "Okay, guys, come here." She tried to hug them, but Eli wouldn't let her.

"You made him mad," he accused. "You made us leave." His voice spiraled up. "I love Matt. And I hate you!" he shouted, and ran down the hall to his room. She could hear him sobbing and wailing, and she shut her eyes. His words ripped at her heart. She wasn't sure what was more up-setting—him loving Matt or saying he hated her.

The hate was temporary. But the love was another matter altogether. She couldn't have that.

When she opened her eyes, Liam was looking from her to the direction of Eli's noise in dismay. She tried to smile, but from the expression on her baby's face she knew she'd failed miserably.

"It will be okay," she said. Liam didn't appear convinced, and frankly, neither was she. Standing up to go talk to Eli, she saw Matt pull in across the street. Her van was in her own driveway; the lights were on. His own house was dark. He looked from his place to hers and she figured he'd realized what had happened. Guilt and something more pooled in her stomach, turning it sour.

She kissed Liam on the head. "I've got to give something to Mr. Matt. I'll be right back. Do you want to stand on the porch so you can see me?"

Liam nodded, so they both went outside.

Matt saw her and waited, but his face was a mask as she hurried up to him. Her whole body trembled, almost as if she was cold. His eyes were completely unreadable and her stomach sank. What had she expected?

"I've got your key," she said, then realized she was gripping it so tightly it was biting into her skin. He held his hand out and she dropped it in his palm, her fingers shaking slightly. "Thank you for letting us stay. I—" She looked up and met his gaze, and just for a second saw the pain there, before the mask dropped back into place.

She cleared her throat and continued, her voice a little rough. "I just think it's best we're back home and out of your hair."

He pocketed the key. "You're welcome." His voice was completely devoid of emotion and it made her wince inside. "But running away doesn't solve anything, Callie."

She stiffened. "I'm not running. I'm getting us out of your way."

He just looked at her. "Sure you are."

It started to rain then, and Callie stood there in the driveway, barely feeling the cold drops mix with the hot tears she couldn't hold back any longer as Matt walked away from her, not looking back. She tried to ignore the feeling that she was making a horrible mistake.

She got Eli calmed down and the kids settled in. She made microwave popcorn, which was a treat, and sat with them to watch a short show on the TV she'd moved out from her bedroom. Both boys were subdued, but Eli no longer seemed angry with her. It was a start, and given how emotionally exhausted she was at the moment, she'd take it. If there were more tears tonight she thought she'd just curl up in the corner and cry herself into a little husk of misery.

Or eat a gallon of ice cream.

After tucking them into bed she sat in her own living room and just felt—sad. Empty. There was none of the relief and lightness she'd hoped to experience. Just the heavy feeling something was terribly wrong. The rain fell outside, a steady thrum on the roof and against the new window. She curled up on the couch and didn't really see what was on the TV. She would put away their stuff tomorrow. Right now she was too exhausted even to move down the hall to her own bed.

She was afraid Eli had been right—they all were in love with Matt. And if so, she'd walked right into the trap she'd been trying so hard to avoid, and landed smack in the morass of pain she'd vowed she'd never feel again.

Matt stared out the window at Callie's house, peering through the rain. Aldo kept padding down the hall to the empty spare bedroom and coming back out, sitting down and frowning at him as if asking, *What the hell did you do?*

It was a valid question, even from a dog, who was clearly smarter than he was. Matt knew exactly what he'd done. He'd scared Callie away. He'd let himself believe—just for a few days— that he could have a place in their lives, even as a friend.

Now he knew better. She was so shut down, she didn't know which way was up, or how to get out of it if she wanted to.

He wasn't sure she even wanted to.

He wasn't the guy to show her, with his crazy lifestyle. He didn't know anything else. But he did know it wasn't good enough. Would she let him see the boys? Or had she decided he was too much of a danger to be around them at all?

His thoughts just circled and made him feel worse.

Her TV was on, but the rest of the house was dark. Was she having trouble sleeping, too? Or was she secure in her own truth that she'd done the right thing?

He thought of her stricken face when he'd turned away from her today. No, she wasn't. But it gave him no pleasure to know it.

He yanked his curtains closed and flopped onto the couch. Tonight would no doubt be a sleepless one. But he wasn't going to spend it thinking about her and what had gone wrong. Nope, he was done with that. He popped open another beer and turned on a basketball game he didn't remotely care about. Aldo made another circuit down the hall and back, then lay on the floor near him with a sigh and rolled his sad gaze up to Matt.

He knew what the old boy was feeling. He lifted the beer and toasted the dog. "It's you and me now, boy."

Aldo just shut his eyes.

CHAPTER FOURTEEN

CALLIE MANAGED TO avoid any sight of Matt for a few days. When she told Maureen she'd moved back in her house, even with the roof and attic not quite finished—and it had taken a lot more effort than it should have to convey it as a good thing—there was the oddest of pauses.

"Why?" her mother-in-law finally asked.

Caught off guard more by her tone than the actual question, Callie scrambled for an answer. "Well, because it was time. There's no reason not to be back here," she stated, echoing what she'd already said. Maybe if she repeated it enough she'd believe it herself. "We needed more space." Not just physical. Emotional. She wasn't getting that, even with Matt across the street. She seemed to feel his presence, or lack of it, all too keenly.

So were the boys.

"There's nothing…nothing between you and

Matt?" Again with the careful tone, with the note of—what? Callie wasn't sure. Maureen didn't sound disapproving, but she couldn't possibly be disappointed, could she? That didn't make sense.

Even though she couldn't see her, Callie shook her head vigorously. "Oh, no. Of course not," she assured her mother-in-law, but she tasted the lie on her tongue. The real answer was yes. But since it—whatever *it* was—was over before it had even gotten off the ground, so to speak, she saw no reason in going there.

Maureen's sigh was audible over the connection. "That's too bad."

Callie nearly dropped the phone. Whatever she'd expected to hear from her, it wasn't that. "What? It is? Why?" Maybe she'd heard wrong.

"I can't think of anyone who'd take better care of you and those precious boys than Matt Bowden," Maureen said firmly. "He's a wonderful man, and frankly, Callie, I think Jason would have approved."

Callie stared out the window. "I—I don't know what to say," she admitted finally. She would never have thought that Maureen and Joe would be okay with her getting involved with another man, much less a friend of their son's. They didn't see it as a betrayal of his memory?

"You don't have to say anything, Callie. We wish—" her voice caught, then picked up speed "—we wish with all our hearts that our son was here. But he's not. You are, and the boys are. You deserve a full and happy life. I can't help but think—of all the places in the world Matt could have moved, it was across the street from you. I don't think that was coincidence. I think this is Jason's way of saying you should finally move on."

Tears streamed down Callie's face. She couldn't have held them back if she'd wanted to. She heard them in Maureen's voice, too. "Maureen. I'm just not sure." She tipped her head up and swiped at her eyes with her free hand, to no avail. "He's not safe. He's such a risk taker."

"Like Jason," Maureen finished, and the understanding in her tone had Callie sinking in a chair.

"No. Yes." Callie squeezed her eyes shut. "He let Eli climb a tree. He went for a bike ride and his friend got hurt, despite all their talk about not running unnecessary risks. I can't take the chance."

"Of what?"

"Going through this again," Callie whispered. Was that wrong? To not want to feel that soul-sucking pain again?

"Oh, honey, there are no guarantees in life. Ever. He could be an accountant who works at home, with no contact with people whatsoever, and then fall down the stairs on his way to do laundry. Tell me this. Would you trade any of the time you had with Jason? Even if you'd known how it would end?"

"Of course not." She wouldn't trade one second of any of it.

"Then I have to ask, why are you fighting it with Matt? Why run the risk—and it is a big one you are taking, Callie—of being alone, with no one, for the sake of not getting hurt? Is being lonely worth it? I can't tell you what to do. Maybe it wouldn't work out anyway, but I saw how he looked at you. And," she added softly, "I saw how you looked at him. Are you in love with him, Callie?"

Callie pressed her hand to her mouth, the tears starting afresh. She knew it was true. Knew it was foolish to deny it anymore.

Maureen continued. "Don't say anything now. But think about it. I believe you owe it to yourself to think it through. Just so you know, Joe and I will support you whatever road you take in the future. We love you and want you to be happy. We know that could—should—involve a relationship with another man. We don't get to pick him for you, Callie, but if we could, it'd be Matt."

Callie hung up feeling as if she'd been run over by a semi. Twice. She hadn't been looking for Maureen's blessing, but felt a lightening in her heart to know that her in-laws were behind her and would honor her and her choices.

She'd been blind. In so many ways.

And yes, she was in love with Matt.

She sank onto the floor. Oh, God.

Did he love her, too? Could she put her heart on the line after how hard she'd tried to push him away? Did she have a choice?

The answer to that was easy. Of course she had a choice. There was always a choice. She could continue to hide and run, and pull her unwilling kids along in her wake, or she could stand up and face these fears and maybe get some semblance of her life back.

It'd never be the same. It wouldn't be the life she'd planned. But to get a second chance at something like this was precious, and she needed to make sure she didn't waste it.

Now all she had to do was convince Matt.

The next day dragged. Callie was pretty sure the clock even stopped a few times, just to aggravate her. She thought she might get whiplash from glancing at it almost constantly. She wasn't completely sure what she was more nervous about: realizing what her feelings were, wondering how Matt felt or deciding that she needed to tell him.

It all added up to a potent brew of sheer raw nerves in her belly.

But she had so much to say to him, and knew she had to talk to him. She owed him, after her behavior earlier. Besides, she couldn't go on in the half-life of loving him and hiding from him. And her kids needed this settled, as well, however it worked out. She and Matt were adults and could act accordingly.

It was a huge risk, putting her heart out there. But the potential rewards were sweet, and life changing for her and the boys. She already knew, even if it all fell through, that she was strong enough to survive.

She hadn't said anything to them yet, wanting to be sure… Well, wanting to be sure. If it didn't work out, she didn't want them to be crushed. Maureen hadn't sounded surprised that morning when Callie had called and asked if she and Joe could take the boys overnight. Her mother-in-law had sounded overjoyed when she'd said they'd be delighted to, even though Callie hadn't said why she needed them to. She hadn't been able to say the words. It was still too private. And maybe it was a way to protect herself in case it all went wrong.

Callie hoped now, several hours later, that Maureen's optimism wasn't unfounded.

Lori smiled at her when they were finally closing up. "Even though you keep denying it, I know you are up to something, girl. Spill. Is it Matt? Did you come to your senses?"

Her blunt assessment made Callie laugh, then just as quickly sober up again. "I don't know. I've decided that I need to talk to him, because what I did and how I handled things wasn't right. Or rational. And he didn't deserve it. How it will go is anyone's guess." She tried to smile, but the butterflies were growing bigger by the minute.

Lori pulled her in for a tight hug. "So you're going to go for it. Good for you. You deserve this, honey. Let me know how it goes." She added a wink as she pulled back. "On Monday, after a weekend of making up with him, of course."

Callie laughed again, but Lori's words brought up a memory of Matt kissing her, and her body gave an unconscious little shiver. Yes, she'd like that. Very much.

She got into her van, but didn't head right home. She'd let Colleen know she'd be a few minutes late. There was something she had to do before she went any further.

Callie pulled into the cemetery and parked. She

took a deep breath and got out. The walk to Jason's grave wasn't far.

She paused on the windswept hill, her eyes on the granite marker in front of her. "Jason Joseph Marshall," read the stone, with his dates inscribed as well.

"Loving son, husband, father."

He'd been all that, and so much more. And now she needed to let part of him go. Callie stood there, head bowed against the wind, eyes damp, but feeling a slowly growing sense of peace.

She hadn't asked any questions, but had her answer.

"Thank you," she whispered to the wind, and kissed her fingers, pressing them to the headstone, letting them linger on the cold granite. "I'll always love you. And our boys will know you. I promise."

She turned and walked back to her car. The rest of her life began now.

The boys were happy to go to Grandma and Grandpa's again. Since Maureen and Joe were going to treat them to dinner at a restaurant, Callie didn't feed them on the way. In the parking lot, she kissed and hugged them, and then Maureen and Joe, too.

"Good luck," Maureen whispered. "He's a smart boy. He'll understand."

"I hope so," she murmured.

The drive back home seemed to take twice as long as the trip there. By the time she arrived, she was shaking and ready to just go hide with that gallon of ice cream she kept threatening herself with.

If he turned her down, she'd go get a carton of rocky road. Tonight. And she'd eat the whole thing.

Not really heartened by that particular prospect, she pulled in her driveway. His house was still dark. She'd noticed he wasn't coming home as early as he had when she and the boys were there, and wondered if he was trying to avoid her, too.

Of course he was. After what she'd done to him? She didn't blame him.

She let herself into the house, turned on a couple lights. She couldn't possibly eat, she was so nervous. She tried to do some cleaning, but kept staring out the window at Matt's house. This was so important. What if she screwed it up?

She gave up trying to do anything, and paced around her living room, rehearsing out loud what she wanted to say. Making sure she hit all the points, that she got it right. So she'd sound smooth, not incoherent and nervous.

Which she was. Terribly.

Finally he pulled into his driveway. She slipped her shoes on and was halfway out the door when another car pulled in behind him. She faltered on the steps, ready to go back into her house. But when Matt turned, she knew he saw her standing there. Even from across the street, his pain mirrored hers, and was nearly palpable. She lifted a hand, and he said something to the occupants of the car—Marley had gotten out—and strode over to Callie. She watched him come, his long stride, his erect bearing indicating his military history, and those intense ice-blue eyes fixed on her as if she were his prey.

Oh, my. It made her joints go liquid.

She seemed to be frozen to the spot, but as

he approached she managed to unstick herself enough to make it down the stairs. He stopped just out of her reach, but close enough she could catch his scent. And see the wariness in his gaze. She wanted to curl into him, tell him she was sorry.

"Everything okay?" he asked, and his voice made her nerves trip.

She could only stare at him, drink him in. God, how she loved him. He must have seen something in her face, because he moved a little closer.

"Callie?"

"No," she blurted, all her carefully rehearsed words falling away. She couldn't have remembered them if her life depended on it. She had to make him see, and quickly, before she lost him forever. "It's not okay. I'm not okay."

He caught her arms and the worry was intense on his face. "Where are the boys? Callie, what's happened?"

She laid her hands lightly on his chest and felt the pounding of his heart under her palms. She was making a total mess of this. "The boys are fine. What happened is I came to my senses."

She dropped her hands and stepped back. If he didn't want her, she was going to let him walk away. If she wasn't touching him, she wouldn't be tempted to hold on to him. To beg him to stay. Goodness, it seemed she had no pride.

He folded his arms across his chest and his arms brushed hers in the process. His expression was still carefully guarded. "About what?"

She peered up at him. It was now or never. She took a deep breath and plunged in. "You were right. About me, I mean. My—fears." His expression softened just a touch, but he didn't say anything. She swallowed and forged on. "I was trying to protect myself from getting hurt again. After Jason died, there was so much pain. So. Much. Pain. I couldn't go through that again. But I kind of shut everything down. It worked for a time, while Eli was little, too. But now—" she took another breath "—now it's not. You showed up and I realized I want—I deserve—more. My kids do, too. A chance to live my life. I want you in it. I've fallen in love with you," she said, and laid it all on the line. "I didn't mean to, but I did." There. She'd said it all. It was up to him now.

He reached out and caught her arm. His gaze was intent on hers, but she couldn't read it. "Say that again."

She blinked. "Um, I didn't mean to?"

He shook his head and moved closer. "No. The part before that."

Before that? *Oh.* Hope bubbled up, just a bit. "I love you." The words were a little soft, so she cleared her throat. "I love you," she repeated, louder, firmly. Wanting him to believe it. Needing him to believe it, especially since she'd made things so difficult for all of them, including her poor kids.

Matt moved a little closer, still holding her gaze, and her breath caught. "Even with my risky job? Despite the possibility that I might get hurt? And you can't control that?"

She swallowed hard but didn't look away. She didn't blame him for his skepticism. "Even with that, Matt." She couldn't help it. She reached up and touched his face, felt the rasp of his five o'clock shadow under her fingers. "I was scared. And you were right, I was—am—trying to control everything. And I can't. I'm going to need some help with that. It won't go away overnight. But I'm not scared of you, or what we could have. But I understand if you don't feel it, too. I'd like you in the boys' life either way, if we can manage it." Her hope fizzled, fell right into a yawning pit in her stomach, when he didn't say anything back. "Okay. Well." She managed a little laugh. Had she misread why he'd wanted her to repeat those three little words? "I guess I'll, um, go back inside now." One carton of rocky road, coming up.

He had her in his arms, and his mouth on hers in a hungry, possessive kiss right there in the driveway, before she could even turn around. For a heartbeat she was startled, then she wound her arms around him, opened to him and kissed him back with every ounce of passion and emotion she had. She wanted to show him, make him feel, how much she loved him. If this was all he had for her, she'd take it.

When he pulled away, there were cheers in the background, and Callie blinked, only then remembering they had an audience. It was Marley and Brice, who were, Callie discovered when she peeked around Matt, leaning up against the trunk of their car, clearly enjoying the show. Marley gave her a double thumbs-up. Matt didn't even turn around.

"I love you, too," he said, his voice rough and emotion shining in his eyes. "You and those boys."

Oh. *Oh.* "Really? Even though I'm a little neurotic?"

He chuckled and pressed a light kiss to her mouth. "Not without reason. But yes, even with that." He turned serious. "I'm sorry I pushed you over Eli being in the tree. That was wrong."

She shook her head and fisted his shirt in her hand, then smoothed it down, the hardness of his chest contrasting with the softness of the cloth. She wanted to pinch herself, make sure this was real. "I needed it. It was so hard to see what I was doing. I was just so focused on not letting anything happen I lost sight of everything else." She wasn't proud of it.

"I'm still sorry." He lifted her chin with his fingers and pressed a light kiss to her mouth. "Where are the boys?"

She swallowed. "With Jason's parents. They—you should know, they approve of this. Maureen basically told me I'd be stupid to let you go."

Matt let out a big laugh. "Remind me to thank her when I see her next." He pulled Callie close. "We're getting an even bigger audience. Should we go inside?"

A glance around showed Colleen on her porch. The other woman gave a little wave and a big grin. Callie felt her cheeks heat. "Oh. Oh, no."

"Your place or mine?" Matt's tone was teasing, but his eyes were serious.

She hesitated, mindful of what might happen as they worked all this out. "Yours."

From the softening in his eyes, she knew he understood.

"All right." He swept her up into his arms and she gave a little squeak and threw her arms around his neck. He was so solid, so warm—and all hers.

"Matt! Put me down. I can walk," she said, laughing.

"It's faster this way," he promised, and strode right past Brice and Marley. "Scram," he told them, and Callie whacked him lightly on the shoulder.

"Be nice," she scolded, but there was no heat in her tone.

"With pleasure," Brice said, and Callie heard the laughter in his voice.

"Don't do anything we wouldn't do," Marley called gleefully, and Callie caught her wicked grin before Matt walked up on the porch, nudged the door open with his foot and carried her through.

He set her on the couch, then sank down beside her. She curled her feet under her as Aldo came up, whole body wagging. She rubbed his head and thought he looked pleased. Maybe even just a little bit knowing.

Matt turned her face to his and she smiled, then her breath caught as she saw the depth of emotion in his eyes. "Callie," he said softly, and picked up her hand. "Are you sure?"

She laid a palm on his face, feeling the slight rasp of his whiskers, drinking in the sight of him, so close. She'd been sure she'd lost him. "I am so sure. I love you."

He turned his head and kissed her palm. "I love you, too." He touched her ring finger. "It nearly killed me the other day when I saw you'd taken your rings off. And I was losing you and couldn't do a damn thing about it." His voice was a rasp.

She leaned into him. It had been hard on her, too. "It was the right time, you know? I couldn't wear them while I felt what I did for you. I'm not ready—" she took a deep breath "—not quite ready to replace them just yet. I will be, Matt. I need a little more time."

He pulled her against him, tucking her head under his chin. "I know that. We'll go at your pace." He hesitated. "You asked me a while ago about my fiancée. Trina."

"I did," she agreed, pleating his shirt with her fingers. The woman didn't have any power over him now. Of that, Callie was certain.

His voice was a rumble under her cheek. "She told me I wasn't capable of letting another person in. That I was completely fine on my own, I didn't need a partner, and that was why I couldn't fully commit to her. I started to think she was right. Not that I wanted to be alone, but I just wasn't cut out for being part of a family. But then you and those cute kids of yours showed up and shot that theory full of holes."

Callie levered up and kissed his chin. "You're welcome."

He laughed a little, then sobered. "But she was wrong. I just hadn't met the right person yet. Because I need you. You and those boys of yours. I want to do right by you. And Jason."

Callie sat back and slipped her hand in his. Matt's words made her heart sing. "You will. We will. He'd want me to be happy, and I think it'd make him happy to know I'm with you."

"Love is a risk," Matt reminded her, but there were finally no shadows in his eyes, or in her heart.

"Bring it on," she answered, and he laughed and leaned in to take her mouth. She wound her arms around him and held on tight, because this adventure was just beginning.

She couldn't wait.

EPILOGUE

Four months later

"PULL IN HERE?" Matt asked as they kayaked toward a sandy, grassy patch off the river.

"Sure," Callie said, and steered her kayak toward the shore. Liam sat in front of her, his chubby little hands gripping the sides of the bright yellow kayak. He'd been mesmerized by the brightly colored dragonflies darting around them, which had helped him not be so leery of the ride.

Eli waved from Matt's kayak. He'd grown in confidence under Matt's careful influence. They all had, really. Last summer Callie wouldn't have put her kids on the water like this, even with the bright orange life jackets they wore. But he'd helped her work to overcome her fears, which meant that, actually, they were all much happier.

"Okay, Liam, sit tight. I'm going to get out and

pull the kayak up on the sand, then I'll help you out, okay?" She dropped a kiss on his downy brown hair as he nodded.

"'Kay, Mommy."

She climbed out and hauled the boat up on the sand. Matt was doing the same thing. They helped the kids out and Callie went back to fetch the small cooler she'd packed with a very basic lunch. When she turned around, Matt and the boys were huddled together. Her lips curved at the sight. Matt, in a navy Out There Adventures T-shirt and colorful swim trunks, looked good enough to eat. He caught her eye and sent her a wink, then stood up and herded the boys over.

"I've got lunch," she said, then stopped and frowned at their very serious expressions. "What? Are we out of bug spray or sunblock? Is someone sick?"

A glimmer of a smile touched Matt's face as Eli shook his head and answered for the group. "No. We need to ask you a question."

Callie's heart picked up. She gripped the cooler harder because her hands were starting to shake. "Is that so?"

Matt stepped forward, took the cooler from her and clasped her hands, his serious gaze never leaving hers. "Actually, I have a question."

Behind him Eli and Liam were jumping up and down, and when Matt went down on one knee, Callie simply forgot to breathe. *Oh, my.*

"I can't imagine my life without you three," he said solemnly, keeping his gaze on hers. But his face blurred as tears started to slip down her cheeks.

"Uh-oh," Liam said, and Callie laughed as she swiped at them.

"Will you marry me, Callie Marie Marshall?" He stuck out a hand. "Guys?"

Eli slapped a box into his palm. "Say yes, Mom!" he said in a stage whisper, and Callie pressed her free hand to her mouth as Matt slid a single, perfect, princess-cut diamond onto her finger. She couldn't even speak to question the wisdom of leaving a five-year-old in charge of the ring.

"Yes," she managed to answer, laughing and crying. And as Matt got to his feet, she threw herself in his arms, while the boys cheered. "As soon as possible," she whispered.

"That can be arranged," he murmured just before he kissed her, tasting like sun and joy and the salt of her tears. Behind them, the cheers turned to gagging.

"They're kissing again," Eli said, disgust in his voice, and Callie pulled away with a laugh. Matt caught her gaze and smiled deep into her eyes.

"Are you sure you want to be a part of this?" she asked, laughing again as Eli and Liam joined them in a huge hug.

Matt pressed a lingering kiss to her forehead, then pulled back just far enough to look into her eyes. "I can't imagine anything better."

As she stood there in the sun, with the three people she loved more than anything, her heart swelled. She tipped her face up to his, sure her joy was simply going to bubble over. "I can't imagine it, either."

* * * * *